An Agreement Among Gentlemen by Chris Owen
Bad Case of Loving You by Laney Cairo
Between Friends by Sean Michael
Bus Stories and Other Tales by Sean Michael
Bareback by Chris Owen • The Broken Road by Sean Michael
Caged by Sean Michael • The Call edited by Rob Knight
Catching a Second Wind by Sean Michael
Cowboy Up edited by Rob Knight
Deviations: Discipline by Chris Owen and Jodi Payne
Deviations: Domination by Chris Owen and Jodi Payne
Deviations: Submission by Chris Owen and Jodi Payne
Don't Ask, Don't Tell by Sean Michael • Faire Grounds by Willa Okati
Fireline by Tory Temple • Galleons & Gangplanks, editor Rob Knight
His Beautiful Samurai by Sedonia Guillone
Historical Obsessions by Julia Talbot • Hyacinth Club by BA Tortuga
In Bear Country by Kiernan Kelly
Jumping Into Things and Landing On Both Feet by Julia Talbot
Latigo by BA Tortuga • Living in Fast Forward by BA Tortuga
Locked and Loaded edited by SA Clements
Long Black Cadillac by BA Tortuga
The Long Road Home by BA Tortuga
Manners and Means by Julia Talbot • Music and Metal by Mike Shade
The Name of the Game by Willa Okati
Natural Disaster by Chris Owen
Need by Sean Michael • Off World 1 & 2 by Stephanie Vaughan
On Fire I & II by Drew Zachary • Old Town New by BA Tortuga
Out of the Closet by Sean Michael • Perfect by Julia Talbot
Perfect Ten: A Going for the Gold Novel by Sean Michael
Personal Best I: A Going for the Gold Novel by Sean Michael
Personal Best II: A Going for the Gold Novel by Sean Michael
Personal Leave by Sean Michael • A Private Hunger by Sean Michael
PsyCop: Partners by Jordon Castillo Price
Racing the Moon by BA Tortuga • Rain and Whiskey by BA Tortuga
Redemption's Ride by BA Tortuga
Riding Heartbreak Road by Kiernan Kelly
Secrets, Skin and Leather by Sean Michael
Shifting, Volumes I-III, edited by Rob Knight
Soul Mates: Bound by Blood by Jourdan Lane
Soul Mates: Deception and Soul Mates: Sacrifice by Jourdan Lane
Steam and Sunshine by BA Tortuga
Stress Relief by BA Tortuga • Taking a Leap by Julia Talbot
Tempering by Sean Michael • Three Day Passes by Sean Michael
Timeless Hunger by BA Tortuga
Tomb of the God King by Julia Talbot
Torqued Tales edited by SA Clements
Touching Evil by Rob Knight • Tripwire by Sean Michael
Tropical Depression by BA Tortuga
Under This Cowboy's Hat edited by Rob Knight
Where Flows the Water and Windbrothers by Sean Michael

This is a work of fiction. Names, characters, places, and incidents either are the product of the author's imagination or are used fictitiously. Any resemblance to actual events, locales, organizations, or persons, living or dead, is entirely coincidental and beyond the intent of either the author or the publisher.

Faire Grounds
TOP SHELF
An imprint of Torquere Press Publishers
PO Box 2545
Round Rock, TX 78680
Copyright © 2007 by Willa Okati
Cover illustration by Atta Vazzy
Published with permission
ISBN: 1-934166-114-3, 978-1-934166-114-1
www.torquerepress.com
All rights reserved, which includes the right to reproduce this book or portions thereof in any form whatsoever except as provided by the U.S. Copyright Law. For information address Torquere Press. Inc., PO Box 2545, Round Rock, TX 78680.
First Torquere Press Printing: August 2007
Printed in the USA
If you purchased this book without a cover, you should be aware the this book is stolen property. It was reported as "unsold and destroyed" to the publisher, and neither the author nor the publisher has received any payment for this "stripped book".

Faire Grounds

Willa Okati

Faire Grounds

Prologue

"The lot of you, get the campsite in order," Horsetail barked. He planted thick fists, no less powerful for the weight of his years, on his hips and glared at the rollicking, tumbling mass of boys wrestling by his caravan.

"Can't you do it?" one lad asked, freeing himself from the tussle. He was young enough to have his front teeth missing, and whistled when he spoke. He'd never grow into the sort of face man or woman alike would swoon over, especially if those jug-ears of his weren't trained to lie flat against his skull.

Horsetail vaguely recognized him as belonging to the Wildwind clan, a particularly poor bunch. The ragged and oversized clothes hanging off the boy's shoulders were a dead giveaway. Flea, was that his name? Wildwinds never did have any sense when it came to what they called their family members, young or old.

No doubt the boy had his own share of work to do with his kinfolk; hard work, but nothing worth having comes for free. Gypsies and other folk of the road knew hard effort was what reaped a man's rewards.

"I've my own affairs to tend to, and I want

to see whether or not you Gypsy younglings are worth your bread and salt. Put this place in order, I said, and I mean every man Jack of you. Clear the brush and rocks, start a fire going -- and you had best know how -- and mind you tend to the horses, too."

"Will we cook something to eat over the fire?" Flea asked hopefully.

Horsetail, his mate Slipstream, and their foster son Lightning had already had their dinner earlier, on the road. They'd eaten a hunk of travel-bread and an apple each, but mercy upon them, boys were all stomach -- a snack would do them no harm. "We'll see," he said, knowing full well he'd be digging in his provisions for treats. Lads needed a firm hand, they did, and Road Lords knew he kept them in line, but he'd not see someone go hungry.

He cast a glance toward Lightning, the boy he and Slipstream had taken into their personal care. His long black hair whipped in ropes around his face as he tussled with one of the scamps, not listening to Horsetail's commands for them to settle down.

"Lightning..." Horsetail growled.

The boy reluctantly let go of his rival. Whereas the other boys had all been playing in fun, Lightning flashed with genuine anger. Welladay, perhaps he'd had cause. Might be the lad he fought had slipped in an insult. One about how this caravan belonged to no tribe, or a nasty word about being raised by two men. Wouldn't be the first time. Horsetail let such comments ride off him like rainwater from an oilskin, but Lightning tended to take those things personal-like.

"Lightning, behave," he chided. "Peace among all of you. I'm for the caravan, but I'll be back soon and I'd better see everything neat as a row of pins when I come back."

The group of boys nodded and gave their word, more or less in chorus. Lightning still crackled with anger, but he gave a jerk of his head to indicate he'd obey.

A good lad, for all his temper. A good lad. And he'd better be, hadn't he?

Horsetail and Slipstream had chosen Lightning to carry on their legacy, after all.

Grunting with the effort -- *curse old bones, not strong as once they were* -- Horsetail climbed into the caravan. Bigger than the usual traveling wagon, they had room for the pallet he and Slipstream shared, as well as a cot up front for Lightning, and all their trade goods neatly stowed besides.

"All well, love?" Horsetail asked gently.

His mate felt the weight of his years more harshly than Horsetail himself, his once-copper hair now gone nearly white, and his limbs thin. Ah, for the days when they were both young and strong, the future stretched out in front of them and the road wide open for their travels.

Slipstream, sitting cross-legged in the middle of their pallet, back straight and proud as any Gypsy in his prime, nodded. "The pain's not so bad now. Good job we ran into that herbalist who knew his foxglove cures, eh?"

Horsetail sighed as he knelt in front of Slipstream. His mate's heart grew weaker by the day, medicaments or no, and he knew they only had a little time left together. Lords of the Road, how it would hurt when the two of them were parted.

But ah, he'd cross that bridge when he had to. In the meantime, he'd enjoy every drop of company Slipstream had to give. He reached out to rub Slipstream's shoulder, the one that ached and gave him trouble. Though Horsetail's hands were big and clumsy, he knew how to offer a decent massage.

Slipstream sighed with pleasure. "Feels good, dearest. There's magic in your touch, there is, how it eases all aches and pains." He stroked Horsetail's long braid, liberally streaked with silver, where he'd tossed the heavy weight over his shoulder to trail on his chest. With a glimmer of his old humor, he gave the locks a tug. "Horsetail," he teased, reminding his lover of how he'd gotten his common name. "You'll be a good father even when I'm gone."

"We'll not speak of such things now." If he had his way, they'd never be discussed at all. "We've gathered a goodly number of boys from the caravans in this Gathering."

"Like flies to honey. Always did happen so with you."

"They'll want some entertainment." Horsetail gentled his touch. "Will you come and join us?"

Slipstream hesitated, then began to cough. A deep, wet sound, the paroxysms rattled his chest and left him sucking for air. All the same, when he could straighten up he did, proud as ever. "I'll be along in a moment."

"Best you rest. No, no, none of your cheek. Stay in the caravan where it's warm. Get near the back -- wrap up snug, if you please -- and you'll be able to see and hear as well as if you were outside."

Slipstream narrowed his eyes, but thank the Lords, he gave way. "Mind you speak loud," he warned. "I'll scold you if you don't, and then where will you be?"

"I'll pitch my voice to carry." Horsetail sealed his promise by leaning forward to drop a light kiss on Slipstream's lips, still soft despite his age. Kisses were about all they could share anymore, but they made those touches count. "Now, I'd best get back outside before those rag-tag lads ruin our campsite."

Slipstream scoffed. "They're Gypsies. They'll have done a proper job."

"Well, we'll see soon enough, won't we?" Horsetail gave Slipstream one more sweet kiss, then backed away to exit the caravan.

The smile on Slipstream's face all but broke his own heart.

Made him gruff when he put his feet on the ground and faced those waiting lads. He snorted as he looked around, pretending to be barely satisfied with the work they'd done. In truth, they'd proved capable as Slipstream predicted. The horses, a light roan gelding and a sturdy black mare with a star between her eyes, were groomed perfectly and secured to a tree with good grazing.

Someone had taken care to remove the Darkflowers, bright pink-and-purple blossoms which Grounders planted as traps for those who lived on the road. Beasts of burden found them irresistible, but they were a deadly poison for true. Horsetail could see their stalks burning in the crackling fire neatly contained within a ring of stones, Lightning watching over the blaze with an eagle's eye.

"You've done well enough," he allowed in pretended grudging approval. "I suppose you've earned your pay."

He felt a hand nudge him from behind, and turned to see Slipstream twinkling at him with some of his old mischief. "The treats you promised," he reminded Horsetail, holding out a bag of brown sugar candies. "A Gypsy's word..."

For Slipstream, his beloved, Horsetail had a grin. He wiped the expression clean as he joined the ring of boys, shoving the packet toward the nearest to him. "Pass it around. One each, mind, and I'll be counting afterwards. Now, you wretches. I'm supposing you want a story, eh?"

To a body, the youths brightened, and not just at the prospect of a sweet. They nodded eagerly, settling themselves into poses of eager listening.

Lightning alone remained crouched in front of the fire, poking the dancing flames with a stick. Horsetail resisted the urge to shake his head in dismay. When Lightning wasn't in a rage, he was far too serious for a boy of his age. Intense, almost frighteningly so.

Horsetail levered himself onto the ground, refusing to make any noise as his joints protested with flares of pain. "A story you'll have, then. I suppose you're wondering why it is Slipstream and Lightning and I travel alone, without kith or kin. Is this the story you want?"

Eyes brightened eagerly. Horsetail and his small family were no small source of wonder to them, they who were firmly part and parcel of thickly clustered clans. "Well enough, then." Horsetail cleared his throat. "I can't tell most of this, as I'm bound by promises I've made, as was my guardian and his guardian and all those who came before. But I'll give you what I can. First off, see our wagon?" He jerked his head back at the caravan. "Aren't many traveling what look like this anymore, are there?"

Curious eyes examined Horsetail's home, no doubt noticing the marks and carvings which dated it to be at least a couple of centuries old. If gossip still flew, as it generally did among the Gypsy clans, they'd have heard how this caravan was enchanted so that it had the weight of a feather and could all but fly over the road, never needing the smallest repair.

One boy, perhaps Flea, whistled. Admiration or dismay, Horsetail couldn't tell. He'd grown accustomed to both reactions.

Not providing any more fuel for those stories, Horsetail didn't confirm or deny their suspicions. No one made the sign against evil; a good omen. "You see what you see. Now, the story of how this came to be."

The boys leaned forward, keenly interested. Lightning didn't take his eyes away from the fire.

But then, he'd heard all this before time and

time again, from when Horsetail and Slipstream first chose him until now.

"Once and once upon a time, and 'twas a time long ago now, there were two brothers. I'll not give you their names, but we'll call them Elder and Younger. Both were born and raised farmers, and, well, Elder was content enough to stay put.

"But Younger, ah, he felt the wanderlust and yearned to travel the road. All the same, he stayed put until a handsome Peddler -- call him Peddler only -- came through one day and knocked on Elder and Younger's door, looking to trade some of his wares -- they were prosperous farmers, after all, you know."

Horsetail warmed to his story. "Younger it was who answered the peddler's knock, and from the moment his eyes and the peddler's met, they knew they were, and would forever be, bound together."

"Magic," one of the lads whispered.

Horsetail inclined his head. "Magic, right enough, which flowed free as water in those days. There's clans out there who still know their way about spells and such -- I've even heard tell of them turning out wizards -- but who's to say if the rumors tell us true?"

He left out the next bit of his yarn, as the boys were too young to hear about how Younger and Peddler had spent every moment they could savoring one another's bodies, lust as well as the true-love magic binding them ever tighter together.

"Peddler should have moved on, as folk from the road are wont to do. But he stayed, didn't he? Couldn't bear to be parted from Younger."

"Would he have left the road for Younger?" a boy wanted to know. The others grew keen with sharpened interest. A Road-man never settled if he could possibly avoid such a thing. He'd be called a deserter, and many would shun him if he didn't have the charm to woo his friends along.

"He might have been tempted," Horsetail allowed, "but no. Younger's itchy feet wanted to roam with Peddler, and so he told Elder of his plans. And ah!" Horsetail threw up his hands. "If I were to tell you how Elder raged, 'twould chill the blood in your veins. But the end's all the same. Younger took his share of their birthright, magic and all, and set off with Peddler to live the life he'd burned for."

"And did they live happily ever after?" one still young enough to believe in such things wanted to know.

"Happily enough. They used Younger's money to buy this caravan, and warded it with the sort of spells one could buy in those days, the best and longest-lasting they could find. When they grew older, they chose an heir from one of the Gypsy clans, and raised him to take their place when they'd grown too old. And so and so on it went, until the line passed to me, as it will pass to Lightning. There! That's the end of my story, and you've had your sweets. Be off with you, now, and mind where and when you tell this tale again."

The boys got up, well-satisfied. A little entertainment, a little candy, and they were happy as horses in green pastures. In small groups or one by one, the bunch wandered off toward their clan's traveling homes, murmuring to themselves about what they'd heard.

Horsetail stayed put, watching Lightning. He didn't speak, but then, he didn't need to. Lightning knew the rest of the story, the ending Horsetail told no one who wasn't adopted into his family.

Elder had placed a curse on Younger as Younger left him behind, using what magic he had left to make the words come true. "A pox on your 'love'!" he'd shouted. "Perversions like the pair of you -- you'll die lonely and without family, and your spirits will be forgotten. Bad luck in this love to you, and may all your travels lead to ruin!"

Younger had been quick of wit, though, and struck back nigh before Elder finished ranting. "When love is true love, it endures, and we will find a line to carry our heritage," he said, shattering that part of the curse.

But he had to temper the rest, for he lacked the power to break Elder's magic entirely. "If those of our line find true love by the time of their twenty-and-first name day, they will be safe from all your damning wishes. With love to carry them along, they will succeed in all they do. True love, the sort Peddler and I share."

He'd slumped in exhaustion after casting the counter-curse, and Peddler had taken his hand to squeeze the fingers. Younger had done what he could, and it would have to be good enough.

They'd make the magic work for them.

But ah, the enchantment Younger used to weaken Elder's curse grew thin these days. Horsetail had been lucky to find his Slipstream, and that in the nick of time. Elder's curse crowded in upon them, and their Gypsy pride would not bear such a thing.

How would Lightning fare, when it came to be his turn?

"Are you well?" Horsetail asked quietly after some time had passed. He knew Lightning would also have been going over the rest of the true story. He also knew Lightning would understand the burden placed on his shoulders.

The boy's eyes flashed with determination and he stuck his chin out. "I can do it," he said stubbornly. "More, I'll find a way to make the magic stronger, make Younger's spells stick hard and fast."

"Don't take too much on yourself, ward. If you can find your one true love, be content."

"I'll do what I've said I will." Lightning returned his gaze to the fire, despite the mutiny in his voice. "You watch and see, Guardian."

Horsetail considered his ward. If anyone could do such a thing, it *would* be Lightning. Near pretty as a girl with his wide, bright eyes and delicate bones and the slim strength he had started growing into, he'd be a fine catch and no mistake.

Lightning would have to be careful he chose the right one, though, of all the suitors who'd be certain to swarm him. If his luck -- the luck Younger had cast on their line -- held, that

Faire Grounds

was.

"Bank the coals," Horsetail said at last. "We're done here for the night. I'm for bed with my Slipstream, and I expect to see you tucking in your bed in three shakes." He stood, hiding his wince at the protest of his muscles. "Good night to you, ward."

"Good night," Lightning responded absently, already moving to obey. A good boy, obedient and dutiful.

Horsetail felt a chill of uncertainty, though, one which didn't fade even when he'd tossed a quilt over his lover and himself, holding Slipstream close. Lightning would have a hard road to travel, fighting to uphold magic near the end of its strength.

A heavy burden to place on shoulders still so young and slim.

But the choice had been made -- as it had been for Younger and Peddler, Horsetail and Slipstream had known Lightning would be their charge from first glance, just as they'd known they were meant for one another -- and what could they do now but prepare their fiery boy as best they could?

Lords of the Road help him, though. *Lords of the Road,* Horsetail prayed, *have a care for my wild storm-boy...*

Chapter One

Ten Years Later:

Once a man had come to the Mossy Rock Faire Grounds, he'd never forget the sight for so long as he lived.

Oh, there were other faires held in all the Kingdoms after harvest or planting or the first signs of the seasons changing, even, but the Faire at Mossy Rock -- well, folk would travel many a mile to reach the edge of the land and partake of the festivities. No faire was so great, nor so packed with merchants and fine goods, and none other offered such rarities as fresh fish or jewelry made from the ocean's bounty.

Traveler liked the celebration as well as any -- in moderation, of course. Not much tempted him off the island he'd chosen as home. Not many understood why he'd settled, and here of all places, at the end of the world.

Well and well, he didn't need their approval; Traveler didn't care what Road-folk and Grounders thought of him. He had his own reasons for living here, and they were sufficient.

The faire had just begun earlier in the

morning, and while townsfolk had busied themselves for weeks getting the faire grounds ready, there was plenty of noise from merchants just arrived; minstrels were tuning their lutes and harps, and the crowds gathered to chat at the top of their lungs.

Traveler blocked them out with the ease of long practice and concentrated on what he was doing.

Or, rather, who he was doing.

Twin Gypsies, just arrived the night before, alike as two peas in a pod in looks and manner. They roamed the road on foot, tinker's packs borne on their backs, sharing and sharing alike in whatever fortune came their way. They'd rented a roomy tent from another clan who had one to spare, and though the townsfolk had ordered Gypsies to camp as far away from their own 'steads as possible, neither cared a whit.

They didn't let much bother them, preferring to enjoy life instead. And oh, how they did, every chance they got. They were old friends of Traveler's, and had beckoned him as soon as he set foot on Mossy Rock's shore.

He'd come, and gladly. The two were a sweet temptation, handsome as devils with their tumbling black hair, now flying about their faces as the three frolicked together, their gleaming dark eyes shut in bliss. Cheerful as a rule, they transformed whatever they chose to do into the grandest of larks.

Traveler approved, which might have surprised some. Folk might call him dark and forbidding, but then, they didn't know him, did they? He appreciated good humor as well as the next man, and having not one but two men to dally with... well, who would turn down a romp such as this?

Lightlaugh, the elder of the two, sat braced on Traveler's lap, one knee to either side of the man's hips. He'd played around a bit, teasing and tempting, but ah, when he got down to business the man put the whole of himself into his entertainment. Wanton as -- well -- the lightdrawers he was, he'd been the first to find one of the flasks of oil the twins carried, and had teased Traveler into getting him ready.

Hardly an arduous task.

Lightlaugh, for all his frequent indulgences with others of like mind, had the knack of working his muscles to stay tight as a virgin. He'd felt like a vise around Traveler's fingers as he'd wiggled the oily digits in. The way Lightlaugh moaned and sighed as his arse was stretched wide was enough to drive any man mad for him. Traveler, as ever, found himself to be no exception.

"Easy, there, that's the way," Traveler crooned as Lightlaugh slid ever so slowly down the length of his aching shaft. "Take your -- ah! -- take your time, friend."

The heat and pressure of Lightlaugh's channel did nothing for Traveler's self-control after nigh on a year without this sort of company. He gritted his teeth and held on to savor the feeling of his prick being swallowed by Lightlaugh's scorching grip.

Lightlaugh tossed his head. "Slow is for snails," he retorted as his arse came flush with Traveler's groin. "I want a good, hard ride."

Traveler grinned. "Welladay, you're in control, aren't you?"

"Too right." Lightlaugh shut up, then, and began to withdraw then spear himself again on Traveler's cock. He keened with pleasure, not caring who might hear. Why not? The twins didn't care.

For that matter, neither did Traveler. Let folk think what they might about the goings-on in this tent.

"Come on, friend," Traveler found strength to bid Fairlaugh, the younger twin. He'd been hovering by Traveler's side, cock hard enough to jut straight out, a bit slick at the tip from not being able to contain himself.

A taste would be grand.

Fairlaugh drew closer. "What would you want?" he teased, already pointing his prick at Traveler's mouth. Almost close enough to lick. "What? Are you interested in this?"

Traveler hissed as Lightlaugh began to rock on his lap, working hard at his self-control. "Yes. Now," he said, the short words all he could manage when his cock was being worked by the older twin's expert arse. "Here."

With a triumphant chuckle, Fairlaugh used his prick to paint a thin line of sooner-seed on Traveler's lower lip. When Traveler licked it off and opened his mouth for more, Fairlaugh eased his way between Traveler's lips. His own parted with bliss. "Such a treat as I've not known in ages."

He had a mouthful and couldn't answer in words, so Traveler used his tongue in other ways, circling the tip of Fairlaugh's cock and driving the point into the slit.

Fairlaugh wailed in pleasure. "More!"

Caught between the twins, Traveler did as he'd been told. He generally didn't care to be ordered about, but when it came to sex, especially with these two, a command or three could be let to slide.

He gulped hungrily at Fairlaugh's throbbing cock, thrust up into Lightlaugh's willing arse, and thought: *this is happiness.*

* * *

Lightning knew he'd be in for a hell of a time from the moment he pulled his caravan up to the edge of Mossy Rock Faire. The last time he'd traveled this far, five years ago, the faire grounds had been wide open to any who cared to come take part in the festivities. The sights and sounds had lent sickening old Slipstream, in the valleys of what would be his final illness, enough strength to sit up and joke with their road kin as Horsetail drove their caravan past. Horsetail had been so pleased to see Slipstream take some new interest in life.

Even then, though he'd just turned sixteen, Lighting knew what was what and had been certain this was Slipstream's last trip to this edge of their world. He'd been right. Slipstream had slipped away the winter following, with Horsetail fast on his heels. Together for so long, they couldn't manage when separated.

On the verge of twenty-one, Lightning still missed them as much as if he'd said his goodbyes only one day before.

He didn't think they'd like the changes come to pass at Mossy Rock.

Heavy gates barred the main entryway with two surly, heavyset guards in position on either side. Men with deep scowl lines and suspicious, ugly looks for Lightning as he drew closer.

They didn't move to open the gates, so Lightning pulled to a stop. Their hateful attitude plucked at his nerves, but he remembered Father Slipstream's advice. With an effort, he put on an attitude of easy good humor. Honey caught more flies, after all, or so Slipstream had tried to teach him.

"Fine afternoon to you," he said pleasantly, choking back what would have been a scowl when the two guards pulled ugly faces. "These are new. Why bar the way?"

One guard spat, a nasty green gob landing near one of Lightning's horses. The beast shied a bit, but a gentle twitch to the reins calmed her down. "Toll," he said shortly. "A silver coin to get inside."

A whole silver? Lords of the Road, that'd be as much as a decent peddler made in a month. Lightning *had* the money, and to spare, but this situation and their attitudes suited him ill.

Still, he'd keep his calm. "A high price."

"Lucky we let you in at all. Damn Gypsy."

"Road-trash," the other snorted. "A silver bit or you'll turn right around and head the other way."

It had been in Lightning's mind to bargain with the pair, but he had good instincts and knew they would gleefully see him on his way. "Very well. A moment, and I'll fetch the coin."

His horses, though he'd not named them, were good beasts and stood still while Lightning loosed their reins and burrowed back in his caravan. A small cache held some of his money -- not all, as it wouldn't do to keep the whole of one's store in one place, lest the loot be discovered by thieving hands. He plucked out a silver.

Things had changed, and for sure. He didn't care for this, no.

While he closed and concealed the cache, Lightning heard the sharp clip-clop of a single horse trotting up to the gates. It, too, came to a stop.

Natural suspicion made Lightning peek out at the new arrival. Golden of hair and pale of skin, he was clearly a Grounder, and one with money, too, from the richness of the velvet tunic he wore.

The guards' expression changed from surly to something almost pleasant. "Come for the faire?"

"I'd a mind to look among the stalls and see if I can find gifts for the lady I've chosen to court." The Grounder's voice had a flat City accent, no music or lilt to his tones. "Why the gates?"

"To keep out what we want kept out. And for them what have to pay a toll."

"Gypsies and the like?" the man inquired, as if he knew his answer.

Faire Grounds

One guard snorted. "Too many damn folk of the road nosing their way 'round here. We're being careful, 'tis all."

Lightning gripped his coin hard enough that the rough edges cut into his palm. His temper, even quick to kindle, flared into life. *Those -- those sheep-spawn! Double-faced cheats!*

He heard the creak of the gates opening. "Enjoy the faire," a guard said. "Good tidings to you."

"And to you." The man on horseback trotted through, free and easy as you please.

Lightning wasted no more time. While the gates were yet open, he scrambled back into his seat and flung his silver bit at the fouler of the two guards. "My toll," he snapped. "Unless you've more to tax a *Gypsy* with?"

The guards' expressions had turned ugly again. They exchanged glances, grunted like the pigs they were, and left the gates open. "In you go. But keep in mind there'll be others like us patrolling. We'll have none of your thieving ways, Road-scum. And you take your caravan to the far end, hear? All the way to the shore, and no closer."

Lightning struggled to hold back an explosion of wrath. He settled for a glare at the guards as he guided his horses and caravan through. What he did not do was let his wariness ease as he navigated through the roadways.

So this was how it would be, would it? Lightning's jaw tightened. *Damn Grounders, anyhow!*

Well, they wouldn't stop him. Let them

try!

* * *

Lying sweat-covered and sated on soft, brightly-colored ground coverings, nestled between the twins, Traveler lazily began to cast his mind around. Lightlaugh and Fairlaugh had had a few stories to tell before they began their romp -- tales of how Gypsies and Road-folk were being treated at this faire -- and he wanted to see why for himself.

Not that he had a care for himself. Folk could think what they liked of him. But when it came to his friends from the road, Traveler thought it wise to get a lay of the land.

He was careful to cover his mental tracks, all the same. It wouldn't do for anyone to suspect they had a wizard in their midst.

Most folk were occupied with their own business, but it took very little effort to sense their rumbling unease and displeasure at the sight of anyone who wasn't a Grounder. Traveler had always been able to pick up on Grounders' suspicion of the Road-folk, but now their distrust ran high as floodwaters.

Well. Traveler raised an eyebrow. Why the sudden tide of loathing? He'd no wish to delve too deeply into how and why, but a word or two for his twins to spread around about extra caution wouldn't go amiss.

He opened his mind's ears a bit wider to better catch what others said, listening specifically for any reference to travelers of the road.

Faire Grounds

"Here comes another Gypsy," a woman complained in a high, shrill voice. Traveler caught a flicker of a vision of the lady as she lay out hanks of embroidery thread in her stall. He risked clinging long enough to see a Gypsy caravan roll past, but could make out no details.

"Thieving bastards, beggin' your pardon for the language," the man working on her awning scoffed. "Keep an eye to your cashbox. Too many of the wretches around this season for my own comfort, and there's the truth."

"It's not so much money I worry about, though there's enough trouble," a third voice piped up. Also female, also Grounder. Traveler couldn't see the dame but imagined her to be fat as a butterball, plump cheeks bunching as she fretted. "'Tis their magic you've got to guard against. Wards aren't cheap, and who's to say they're enough?"

"Dangerous, dangerous folk. We've been shown the light, so we have, and protect ourselves though we may, there'll be trouble before this faire's done. You mark my words," said the man.

Traveler had heard enough. More than a few words in his twins' ears, then, and a stern warning for them to spread among the Gypsies and other folk who lived on the road. He dismissed his spying with disdain, a nasty taste in his mouth. Just a bit more idling with his twins, and he'd get to work...

"Ho, there! Ho, the cursed Gypsy wagon! Get down from there, trash."

Now *there* was a foul tone, and no mistake.

Traveler sat upright on instinct, ignoring the way his twins grumbled.

"Get down, I said!"

Traveler hesitated. He didn't like to get involved, but for a reason he couldn't name, this challenge made him edgy. Impulsively, he found his trews and stepped into them, then made for the tent-flap and took a curious look outside.

A brute of a man, the kind some folk would think handsome with his Grounder-yellow hair and his broad features, had blocked a caravan's way at the edge of where Gypsy-folk camped. A group of other Grounders, likely this one's friends, stood some short distance away, snickering without bothering to hide their cruel-sounding mirth. "Do you climb off that witch-touched cart, or do I come up to drag you myself?"

The driver of the caravan looked up, and Traveler nigh lost his breath.

By the Lords of the Road, he had *never* seen a man so comely. Hair sleek and black as one of the prized otter pelts bound in a woven braid that reached past his lap, with stubborn curls springing free. Curls a man could ache to wrap around his fingers. Wide eyes, dark as were other Gypsies', but Traveler could see the fire blazing in them from the way this youth sat stiffly upright, hands knotted around the reins he held.

"Out of my way," the driver barked with the thinnest thread of mastery over a temper anyone could hear crackling, ready to burst open. "I've had enough of you Grounders and your insults. Move, or I run you over."

"Ha!" The chief Grounder tossed his head like a stubborn gelding. "You daren't. Hurt a one of us, and you'll not just be barred from the faire forever and ever again, but you'll find yourself beaten, then put in the stocks. 'Tis the *rules*, they are, and there's guards all about who'll see justice done." He paused, a sly look crossing his face. "But I could overlook your rudeness, I could. Climb down and walk with me to a secret place I know."

The driver jerked with fury. "You had best not be suggesting what I suspect," he warned. "As if I'd willingly go anywhere with a Grounder, much less let him touch me with such clammy hands as yours!"

The Grounder laughed, an ugly sound. "You'd rather I reported you for insolence, then? Climb down and make up your insults to me. Might even be a little gift in it for you, if you treat me right. There's a tale or two about how Gypsies have a few skills worth trading for. Your sweet mouths, for one." He groped himself rudely. "Your choice, road-scum."

Enough was well enough. Even if the Gypsy weren't the loveliest lad Traveler had ever laid eyes on, he'd be damned if he'd see a one of the Road-folk forced into this kind of humiliation.

Shirtless and bootless, Traveler emerged from his twins' tent and made his way toward the confrontation. He kept his walk casual and careless, as if the fuss made no difference to him one way or another. But when he reached the Grounders and the wagon, he came to a stop. "What's the problem?"

His inquiry, though mild, drew the Grounders' attention around. No one knew of his powers -- of that he'd made certain -- but he was tall as an ox with the lean muscles of a panther. He could beat them to a jelly without half trying, but it was the superstition bred into them of a man like him that made them pull back.

"No trouble," the lead Grounder muttered. "Just havin' a chat with this one, s'all. Friendly-like."

Traveler managed not to roll his eyes. Instead, he laid a hand on the caravan -- the once-powerful touch of enchantments startling him -- and looked up into the driver's face.

Lords, he could die happy looking at that face. Delicate and fine-boned as one of the fey from stories of old, but fierce with rage, not to mention stubborn and proud enough for three of his kind. He wouldn't own up to how the Grounders had been tormenting him, Traveler knew, and he wouldn't push.

"Best be moving along, then," he suggested with a shrug. "You lads have work to be done, don't you? A wise man would hop to, then. There's plenty of money can be made by willing hands turned to labor."

The lead Grounder mumbled something half-vicious and half-wary, but after a moment of looking torn, he spat in disgust and turned around. His cronies followed, casting looks over their shoulders and making the sign against evil.

Let them; Traveler didn't care.

Returning his attention to the Gypsy,

Faire Grounds

Traveler expected to see a grin of thanks, and perhaps hear a quip or two about how the damned Grounders needed to be put in their places.

Instead, he found himself faced with double the fury this Gypsy had turned on his former foes. "Take your hand off my caravan," he snarled. "Who gave you the right to come barging in? I needed no help."

"I'd be a poor specimen of road blood if I stood by and listened to such muck being hurled. I only meant to help."

"Keep your mind set on your own business from now on." The Gypsy gathered up his reins. "I can take care of myself."

Of that, Traveler had no doubt.

Didn't mean he didn't crave the chance to get closer to this one, though.

But on a third hand, he knew enough to back away before this wildcat of a man jumped down from his driver's seat to tackle him. Traveler knew he himself would come out on top, but one such as this would bite and scratch. "I'm called Traveler," he offered. "What would you be called?"

"My name is none of your affair. Step aside, and this is the only time I'll be asking."

Oh, but this youth's temper lit him up from the inside like a torch, eyes blazing and face flushed. Traveler felt himself immeasurably tempted to climb up and touch his mouth to those sweet lips, to see if they were soft as they looked. To wind that braid around his wrist and pull the Gypsy close...

He must have betrayed his thoughts

somehow. The Gypsy snarled at him, well and truly enraged by Traveler's interest. "Leer at me, will you? I'm no more tempted by you than those clumps of Grounder horse droppings. Move!"

That put him in his place, didn't it? Traveler stepped aside obediently. Growling with anger, the Gypsy flicked his reins and set the horses walking forward -- slowly enough for Traveler to trail his hand along the side of the caravan and taste its magic like a rare wine.

Lightning, he knew in a flash. *His name is Lightning. It suits. He's lived alone for a long and long time, and likes it that way. Yet there's something... something odd...*

Traveler flexed his hand. He'd felt a bit of a tingle there, something he'd never sensed before. Odd.

Well, then, like it or not, and little as he still cared to get involved in any of these goings-on, he'd be keeping watch over this one.

He felt a...tie to the young Gypsy.

Peculiar.

* * *

Lightning drove forward, steady as he went although his head was all a-whirl with what had just happened.

Bedamned if he hadn't felt Younger's enchantment take firm hold. Bedamned!

He knew: he'd met his life-mate in this Traveler.

This busybody who'd stuck a beaky nose in Lightning's own business. Who raised the hair on his neck in irritation and kindled his temper like bellows to a flame.

Life-mate to a man he already despised.
Damn!

Chapter Two

Hard work, Horsetail had told Lightning often and oft, *is the cure for whatever plagues your thoughts.*

At which point Slipstream, canny as Horsetail, would nod his silver head. He added nothing, but he didn't need to. Slipstream's silences were effective as a thousand words. And as a boy, the words rarely spoken as a reprimand for whatever had sparked his temper were a good enough cure.

Which is why, Lightning thought as he struggled with a heavy carved chest, *I'm out here churning up a muck sweat instead of going back and pounding those Grounders' spotty faces for them.*

Or thinking about Traveler.

Trying not to think about Traveler.

Lightning stopped with a huff of breath and examined what would have to do as his shop front. In times past when the Mossy Rock Faire had been a haven, not a pit of snakes, they'd have given him ample space to spread out with a proper booth and perhaps a cushion or two for customers to sit on.

He suspected he was lucky enough they'd let him sell out of his caravan now. Which he

Faire Grounds

would be forced to. He'd learned right quick there were no places among the merchant stalls-to-let for Gypsies, and not even the lure of extra money would ease his way in where he'd have a hope of making any decent profit at this faire.

But damned if he'd let them get the best of him. No, Lightning would depend on word of mouth, letting the Gypsies and Road-folk come to him, and perhaps it would go from there to ears ever keen on hearing gossip. Then they might come. Suspicious of him, to be sure, but eager enough for the goods he traded to venture to his caravan.

Lightning wrestled the chest he'd lifted into a nice grassy spot by one caravan wheel and sat down on top, wiping perspiration from his forehead and blowing out a chuffing breath. He tried to concentrate on business.

So many crates already unloaded -- they'd be safe enough left out, for Gypsies and Road-folk did *not* thieve, as Grounders believed -- yet so many left to go. He began adding them up in his mind, but somewhere between six and seven he flashed back on a mental image of Traveler and lost count.

If Lightning had been looking a-purpose, he couldn't have found a man who suited him better -- physically. Traveler stood tall and broad as a young oak, but hadn't such a size to inspire fear. Unless he wanted such a reaction, or so Lightning suspected. Smooth dark hair and black eyes marked him as a Gypsy, and so did the tent he'd come from. Lightning, who missed very little, had peeked inside the open flap and seen two naked young Gypsies tangled up together on knotted sheets. Lighting had recognized the smell of a familiar scented oil that spoke volumes of what exactly Traveler was doing with those two young Gypsies.

Lightning's hands, which had been counting on his fingers, fell between his knees. He might be young, but he was no innocent. The things a man like Traveler could do would be endless. He had the air of a practiced lover around him, experience glowing in his aura and eyes. Ah, such a heated gaze as he'd looked at Lightning!

In that look, Lightning had seen all Traveler wanted to do with him without knowing so much as his name. He'd have had the twin Gypsies kicked out of their tent and drawn Lightning inside. Stripped off his clothes with skillful hands, using his fingers to stroke down honey-colored flesh where no man had touched Lightning before. Guiding Lightning through the steps of how to get a lover undressed without fumbling.

Traveler would stand naked before him, gazing at Lightning with the same wonder and delight he'd shown before, all the while waiting for Lightning's own response.

Lightning moaned softly at the thought. Traveler would be toughly muscled as a stallion -- oh, there was a comparison for you, if you pleased. Solid in only the way a hard-working man could be. Tempting, so very tempting. Lightning would want to touch, and Traveler would invite him to, but he would take more time to look his fill first.

He'd have scars. Lightning wasn't sure how

he knew, but he felt certain. Those solid chest muscles and ridged stomach would bear the marks of old slashes. From swords? Daggers? Both? A past full of danger, then, but life was never safe on the road.

And his cock, it would be a thing of beauty. Hard with lust, it would jut out in front of his lean hips with clear intent. Lightning had caught glimpses of erections before, but never had one been so brazenly displayed for his approval.

It would be so easy to reach out and touch Traveler's twitching length. To run his fingers over the man's cock and test to see how different this man's organ was from his own. Soft. Hot. Huge.

Demanding to be serviced.

Lightning's mouth all but watered at the notion of Traveler leaning back and guiding Lightning between his legs. Lightning would kneel, tossing his braid out of the way, and Traveler would guide him through what pleased best when one man laid his mouth on another's cock. He'd be a patient teacher, coaxing his student on with soft words and gentle touches, and love every second of the lesson. Make his pupil lust after more teaching.

He would hear the groans of satisfaction from both throats. Lightning shuddered as his cock, which had risen while he dallied over thoughts of Traveler's body, demanded his attention.

Lightning let one hand cup his cock through the weathered trews he wore, rubbing just hard enough to set up a delicious tingle. He had to duck into the wagon to ease his condition; he'd savor the rest of what he could imagine.

Half-closing his eyes, Lightning flashed on a picture of a design inked into Traveler's stomach, just above where the trail of hair led to...much more interesting things. He held off looking down, though, all the better to examine this tattoo. They weren't common decorations for Gypsy or Grounder alike, as the inks were costlier than a year's wages. He couldn't make out the details, but thought he saw a curved knife, a red, red rose, and the light of a candle on...what was that...a skull?

He jerked out of the vision with a gasp. True-sight or not, these occasional glimpses made Lightning uneasy. Slipstream had had the Gift of being able to foretell the future, and didn't fear what might come, but Lightning couldn't help feeling a queasy uncertainty. A vision meant one of the Lords of the Road were touching your mind, and wasn't that a thing to be cautious of?

Even though all-too-precious time was fleeting by, Lightning stayed put. Traveler was a thought he couldn't toss aside.

Life-mate. How in the hells?

It made no sense. Hadn't he heard Horsetail and Slipstream talking time and time again about how once their eyes had met, both had known for certain they belonged to one another? He'd seen no such recognition in Traveler's gaze. Only curiosity, pity he didn't want, and something Lightning couldn't identify but made his muscles tense with wariness.

Had he not felt the link form? Lightning was fairly sure Traveler hadn't. Was this all his own imagination, then? Or was, perhaps, the magic growing too weak for this use?

Ach, ach, such thoughts hurt Lightning's head. He got up, determined to get to work and keep going until he collapsed with exhaustion and no more energy to think. His swollen cock had gone right down after his vision of the tattoo, which was well enough; saved him the time he'd have spent on stroking his prick inside the caravan.

As if his very mind taunted him, he had another thought of Traveler's face, Gypsy through and through, sharp as a hawk's. And of his broad hands, and nearly lost control as he dreamed about them sweeping his body. Admiring. Savoring. Teaching. Worshipping.

Work, bedamn you! Lightning ordered himself. Stubborn, he reached for another crate and hauled the heavy box toward him. He'd not think any more about being life-mate to a man who'd humiliated him yet brought him low with lust.

He'd drive that man right out of his head.

For the time being, at least.

As long as he could.

* * *

Traveler could step lightly as a mouse and unseen as a passing shadow when he so desired, which he did now. The urge to follow young Lightning bothered him more than a bit. All

Traveler wanted out of life was to be left alone, yet he felt compelled to track this lovely Gypsy's steps and keep an eye out for his well-being.

Magic? For the first time in his adult life, Traveler wasn't sure. He'd felt a tingle of something odd when facing Lightning down, and when touching his wagon, but the old and fading enchantments were not ones he happened to be familiar with. And Lightning wasn't the one wielding them; Traveler would have bet his dust-covered wizard's staff on the question.

Staffs... oh, aye. Traveler had a particular "stave", though he disliked the pretty words of fainting maidens for the plain thing, quivering in his trews, desperate to plow those tight arse cheeks or plunge between Lightning's tender pink lips. He craved this man like water, but Traveler put the urge down to good old-fashioned passion, not magic. The Gypsy Lightning was far too pretty for his own good, probably all unaware -- ah, but he could get himself into deep trouble without taking precautions -- and such a sweet temptation that Traveler could not help but pursue the youth.

He hated getting involved in the affairs of other folk. Why, then, did he feel such a strong impulse to take Lightning under his protection?

Magic or no, he'd work the issue out. Such things could take time, though, and he chose not to waste any precious moments on indecision.

He followed Lightning because he could, because he wanted to, and because he couldn't turn away.

"Where will you lead me next?" he whispered soft as a breath of wind, certain no one would hear him. "Fiery Lightning, where will you strike?"

* * *

Lightning stood and stretched. There, he had his cargo unloaded. Precious as gems, every ounce, but safe among his fellow men.

The bright sun had long since passed noon, and was heading toward the horizon, red as a ruby. He'd had a lengthy day, so he had, and if he was sensible, Lightning knew he'd be setting up a campfire and figuring out what to eat for dinner. Walking among the caravans and greeting old friends of Horsetail and Slipstream.

Instead, he found his bare feet turning toward the part of the faire grounds he'd been warned against. Anyone with a drop of sense wouldn't poke this lion with a stick, but Lightning burned against all commands to the contrary of what he desired.

And he wanted to see the faire for himself.

Surely those foul guards wouldn't arrest a Gypsy out for a simple stroll?

Welladay, he'd take his chances.

Lightning set off at a leisurely pace, hands tucked in his pockets, striving to appear casual and careless. No one paid him any mind until he exited the grounds set aside for Road-folk, but once stepped outside -- Lords of the Road, he felt like a mouse under the piercing gaze of a hundred vicious owls.

He set his jaw stubbornly and walked on. The Grounders might have stared, pointed, and whispered behind their hands or openly snorted, but they'd not hurt him or made any threats. He'd just see how far he could get.

Not idle, Lightning used his eyes to drink in everything possible while he walked. The faire seemed blander than usual without Gypsies blending in, their lack of bright colors and gaiety leaving all else dour and dowdy. The flat accents of Grounders made him miss the Gypsy lilts he preferred, and their dull appearances could not compare to the vivid life in a roaming man's face.

"Welladay! So there you are!" A hand seized Lightning by one arm. "Truth, I thought we'd be on the hunt for days."

Lightning stiffened and whirled around, as whoever this was had approached him from behind. He wished for a second that he'd thought to bring a dagger -- but relaxed as soon as he saw the young woman who'd accosted him, all bright red curls and mischievous green eyes.

Nell, one of the few Grounders Lightning had some use for. Her holding was small, but she always offered shelter and what food she could spare to any who happened to be passing through. Lightning had traded with her several times, his own wares for her herbalist remedies, and they'd developed something as close to a friendship as he could manage.

Faire Grounds

Nell, ever the chatterer, didn't give Lightning a chance to speak. "And aren't you a balm for sore eyes? Healthy and hearty as always, though the state of your clothes... Lightning, Lightning, when will you learn your way around a needle and thread, or think to barter for patch-work?" She *tsked,* plucking at one fold and another of Lightning's admittedly shabby shirt.

"I've better for when I need a show," he said, pulling loose. Lightning didn't care for hands, friendly or no, tugging him about. "This suited me today."

"I would assume he had much work to do. Hence, he wears what he can afford to get dirty." The crisp yet musical voice came from behind Nell. "Greetings to you, Lightning, son of Horsetail. You have grown into quite a man since we last met."

"Lightning, you know Meilin." Nell gave Lightning a nudge. "Such luck, to meet two old friends within the space of one hour!"

Lightning inclined his head to Meilin, who gave him a small nod in return. Unlike the Gypsies Lightning belonged to and the Grounders Nell had sprung from, Meilin was...a mystery. He stood at least a head shorter than Lightning, who could boast no great height. He wore his hair cut short about his face, deceptively young with its slanted black eyes and smooth dark-saffron skin. No one really knew how old Meilin might be, and Lightning knew better than to ask.

Meilin kept his own counsel on everything. If he chose to speak, the person he addressed had better pay attention, even if his rhymes and riddles were like to drive a man mad more often than not.

"I have grown," Lightning allowed. "And I am a man now."

"As I see; so do others," Meilin replied, then drew back and plunged his hands into the sleeves of his brightly embroidered scarlet jacket, unlike any garment Gypsies or Grounders alike wore. There were tales of men like Meilin who lived beyond the snow-covered mountains no one could pass, who lived forever and a day and ate wisdom as their only food.

Some considered them fairy stories.

They had not met Meilin.

His greetings apparently concluded, the slight man turned and began to walk away, decorated slippers making no noise on the soft grass of the faire grounds. Nell huffed in dismay. "And there he goes again. Lightning, will you forgive me? Needs must I follow him, for he's promised me a trade of fine thread for a stock of curative powders. We'll meet again soon, and there's my word."

Lightning felt amused at the way Nell fluttered like a mother hen. Few to none had shown him such affection since Horsetail and Slipstream passed on. Could it really have been so long as five years ago? Was he really so old as twenty-and-one years? It felt like much less time had passed, and yet like much more at the same time. Memories were chancy things. Although Lightning had preferred, even before Horsetail and Slipstream left, to keep himself

Faire Grounds

to himself, more often than not he found Nell's company to be... pleasant.

"Of course." He bowed to her. "You know, I think, where I can be found?"

Nell made a face. "Those silly new rules. Someone should knock a bit of sense into Mossy Rock's leaders. But aye, I know, and I'll be by tomorrow. Fare you well!" She took off after Meilin, who despite his sedate pace had gotten a good distance ahead. Lightning watched with an internal chuckle until they disappeared.

And it was then he began to hear the chattering around him. Oh, the Grounders didn't appreciate a Gypsy talking to one of their own, and as for what they thought of Meilin? They might as well call him a devil and be honest.

Three women manned what looked to be like a bakery stand directly across. Old and grey, they were the sort that grew sharper with age. Their narrow faces were pinched with disdain and they didn't bother to keep their querulous voices down.

"Such a nerve!" The lady sniffed with disdain. "But then, not a one of them obeys a rule that doesn't suit them, do they? Look at this blot of scum floating about as if he owned the whole pond. I've a mind to call the Guards, I do."

"Surely someone already has," one of her fellows said, eyeing Lightning with the same disgust. "They'll be here any minute to take him off to the stocks."

"More than he deserves, the filthy thief."

Lightning's ever-ready temper flared. He kept still, though, pretending he heard nothing and was merely enjoying the warmth of the descending sun.

Although if he *did* hear the threatened Guards coming, he'd be off like a rabbit. No matter how hot his head, Lightning considered himself no fool and he didn't have a mind to be trussed up in stocks.

Another vision, all-unbidden, flashed across his mind's eye: himself, bare of any stitch, laid out on what looked and felt like a wealth of bright, down-filled pillows. His arms were stretched tight above his head, wrists bound tight to something he couldn't see. Both his legs had been parted and fastened as well, securing him firmly in place.

He felt no fear, though. Traveler knelt between Lightning's spread knees, a sly look on his face as he trailed an oil-slicked finger down Lightning's belly. The heat of his touch made Lightning gasp and his stiffened cock jump.

"Such a good boy, trusting yourself to me this way," Traveler crooned. "You'll love this, I swear."

Lightning believed him. He trembled and arched, desperate for Traveler to hurry up, to touch him where no man had before, to *thrust* his fingers deep inside...

"What is he, in a fit?"

The puzzled snipe of one of the biddies brought Lightning out of his vision. He fought with himself to conceal his dismay. What were the Lords of the Road playing at, showing him these things?

And by their might, be damned if he hadn't raised wood from his vision.

Thankfully, the Grounders didn't notice. Sweet mercy, what they might think or accuse him of if he were caught being aroused in their midst...cursed visions!

"More like trying to put us at ease so he can slip in and filch a trinket or two," he was dismissed with scorn. "Well, we'll keep a sharp eye on him until the guards have come. But while we wait, can you guess what I've heard from the chandler's wife today?" The lead harridan dropped her voice into a sly whisper -- which Lightning found he could hear with ease. More magic?

"I've not seen her in ages. What news?"

"Yes, yes, what news?"

"Traveler's off his island," the biddy cackled. "And not just for a visit, either, as he's wont to do. He's been walking the faire grounds all this day long."

"No," her friend breathed. "What brings him off his rock of an island, Hettie?"

Hettie tossed her head like a persnickety mare. "There's no word on his plans yet," she admitted grudgingly. "Not that I trust him an inch, I don't!"

Lightning found himself listening keenly. What, he wondered, did others think of this mysterious man?

"He's naught but trouble on two legs," one of Hettie's cronies agreed. "Just like a Baba Yaga. I swear, milk curdles in its churns and dogs howl for fear when he ventures into town."

"Don't believe a word they say," a heated voice whispered in Lightning's ear. Traveler! He turned round about quickly as he could, but saw no one. Not even anyone departing in haste.

His spine prickled as it always did in the presence of magic. Yet another reason to dislike Traveler -- yet Lightning was bound to the man, wasn't he?

Ach, what a conundrum.

"Best he stay out on Starling Rock," Hettie said decisively. "I'll get my man to put in a word at the next Council meeting. Retired from the road or no, I'll not sleep easy in my bed at night until he's been reined in."

Retired? A Gypsy choosing to live as a Grounder? Lightning's heart sank in dismay. Oh, surely not! His true-mate couldn't be a deserter. He wouldn't be able to bear such a fate.

"Any other news?" Hettie's friends twittered excitedly.

Hettie's mouth twisted down. "Nothing to speak of. He never says one more word than he has to -- but who knows what he's cursing in his silence? And when he does talk, I can't make out half of what he says. And do you know, rumor has it he said once how he can't understand the way *we* talk!" She huffed. "Now Cora, Sadie, have you ever?"

"Never. And there's something deep wrong about that, there is. Mayhap he speaks with demons and that's his native tongue."

"I'd not doubt it, Sadie. He's a darksome

Faire Grounds

sort." Hettie made the sign against evil, not bothering to be discreet. "Bold as brass, too, and I'll never understand why the Council let him purchase a homestead even on that bit of an island. And retired from the road? Retired, my right foot. The Gypsies love that road of theirs like hogs to slop."

"He must have something to hide, keeping to himself that way. Do you think –" Sadie's voice dropped to an excited whisper – "do you think he's on the run?"

Hettie took up the idea eagerly. "Robbed a rich man, perhaps?"

Sadie clutched her chest. "Wanted for murder, could be?"

"Put nothing past the Traveler," Hettie said with a sage nod. "Sounds likely to me he'd have stolen all the money he'd have needed to buy that island, no small sum." Hettie tapped her forehead knowingly. "There's something to him, I just know that. And we'll get to the bottom of whatever he's hiding, so we will."

The three dames twittered in agreement.

Lightning seethed. To the hells with all Grounders and the nasty workings of their minds! No matter how he felt about Traveler, good or ill, and never mind what -- else -- was passing between them, the man needed to be warned.

But where to find a man who seemed able to vanish into thin air when he didn't want to be seen?

He'd start with the Gypsies, Lightning decided. One of them might know how to locate Traveler. He squashed a flutter of excitement in his stomach at the thought of seeing Traveler again in the flesh. The strong, hard flesh which had him quivering like a colt, hungry for treats from gentle-seeming hands...

Bah! Lightning did an abrupt about-face and stalked back through the winding pathways of the faire. This time through the Grounders were bolder, calling out taunts and even offering up threats, but although they stung his temper he paid them as little mind as he could.

Nothing -- nothing -- made him angrier than a group of bullies setting their sights on an "easy" mark to prove what big men they were. Not that Lightning thought Traveler would go down easy; oh, no. He'd be the type to fight back and fight well, but one person could only do so much against a horde out for blood.

And you want to spare Traveler any harm, a voice whispered inside Lightning's mind. *You want to keep him safe and sound, and lure him to your bed...*

Lightning gritted his teeth and walked faster, as if he could escape his own thoughts. Nearly to the Gypsy encampment, now, not much farther. He'd just stop by his own caravan for a moment to gather his breath and then --

He froze. Lords of the Road! This couldn't be.

Grounders, two of them, a massively fat old lady and the same wretch who'd threatened Lightning before, both digging in Lightning's trunks of trade goods. Cackling to themselves as they gathered up packets of his valuable

Faire Grounds

property, and not a care for who might see.

But come to that point...

The Road-folk in the wagons roundabout seemed to take no notice of the thieves in their midst. Men stretched out on the grass, women busied themselves with setting up camp, and children ran about in wild abandon.

No one saw the robbers.

Magic! Lightning shook with rage. Putting up wards against one's own stall, well, he could cope with those. But to be such hypocrites that they'd steal from those *they* accused of being scoundrels and thieves?

Lightning flew at the pair, shouting at the top of his lungs. His yell drew the attention of the other caravans even as he grabbed both Grounders by their collars. They kicked, yelled -- and their enchantments popped as would soap bubbles.

The bloated old woman hugged purloined goods tight to her bulging belly. She spat at Lightning. "We're only taking back a little of what's been robbed from us over the years."

"Way we figure, whatever we want is ours right and proper," the male wretch boasted. "Won't any Guards stop us from taking anything we please, either. And if you lay one finger on us to cause harm, you'll be strung up for the birds."

Lightning forced himself to halt, hands curling into tight but useless fists. Damn them, they were probably right. The whole of the Grounders and the rulers of the faire would back this pair up, and the others who'd flood in after them.

Now he knew why Gypsies had been allowed inside at all. They were sources of treasure to be plundered, nothing more. The faire's idea of a joke!

"Nah, then, that's not such a good idea," a familiar voice remarked. Traveler stepped up next to Lightning's side easily as if he belonged there by right. "Why don't you put those goods down and move along? The Gypsies aren't worth your trouble otherwise, are they?"

He spoke gently, but Lightning felt the undercurrent of enchantment being woven through his words. Did anyone else sense it, too, or was it because they'd been tied together that he could tell?

And how it burned, to hear one of their own putting him and his kin down!

The old woman paled, but the young man sneered. He dropped his loot with a sneer. "Tainted by Gypsy rot, anyway," he scoffed. "Come on, Grandmer. Leave be. Nothing worth having here."

Lightning felt a slight relaxation in Traveler's muscles as they watched the two swagger and waddle away.

He said nothing until they were out of sight, and the other folk of the road chattering to each other in worry.

Then, Lightning kicked Traveler hard as he could in the shin. "What the *hells* are you playing at?"

Traveler swore and jumped back. "You were looking for me," he gritted. "I come to find you, and I lend you my hand, and this is the thanks I get?"

Looking at him made Lightning's stomach churn with lust and doubt and suspicion. He kept their gazes locked, but used a trick Slipstream had taught him to keep his personal feelings hidden behind a cool blankness. "I can take care of myself."

"I meant no offense."

"You've offered it and then some." Lightning's temper had been tried too many times already in one day. He'd passed the point of being rational. "The next word you're going to say is 'goodbye', or we'll see who comes out on top in a tussle."

Traveler's look turned dangerous. "Are you really wanting to find out? Lords of the Road, but you're a prickly little porcupine despite your sweet looks."

Insult to injury. Lightning pointed away from his caravan. "Go!"

Traveler looked first as if he'd like to turn Lightning over his knee, then shrugged with an easy, feline grace. "Just as you like, then. More the fool me for getting involved." He sounded disgusted. "Enjoy your stay at the faire, Prickles."

He stalked away. Lightning cursed himself and damned his own eyes for eagerly drinking in the long, tough lines of Traveler's body -- and his mind, too, for aching to see him bare, from wanting to run his hands over the man from head to foot.

Lightning could read men, in his way, and from the set of Traveler's shoulders he deduced the Gypsy to have washed his hands of Lightning. And his temper had kept him from delivering the warning.

Hells, he'd have to go after the man again -- even if he didn't know the life-mate enchantments wouldn't push them in one another's paths.

The thought made Lightning grind his teeth. They'd meet again, they would.

And if they didn't kill each other, he'd have to figure a way to tell Traveler about the enchantment binding them -- and soon, for time was running out.

Now, wouldn't that be a fine old time?

Chapter Three

Against his better judgment, Traveler did *not* storm to his boat moored on the stony beaches of Mossy Rock and head straight for his welcoming, comforting island home as he desired. Instead, knowing Lightning would be watching him suspiciously, keen as a hawk, he stalked around the corner of a caravan, safely out of sight, then kicked at the innocent cart's wheel with a savage curse.

Bedevil the young Gypsy, comely as he might be! No one had gotten so deep beneath Traveler's skin in ages upon ages, and he'd been determined that no one ever would again. Yet what did Lightning do but slip beneath his defenses like fire through a reed, and set to needling him half out of his wits?

Aye, and there had to be something going on beyond what his eyes could see or magics could ferret out. The strange enchantments clinging to Lightning were at the bottom of Traveler's unwilling fascination, to be sure. Well, he'd see those undone. He was *Traveler;* he answered to no man, and he walked alone. No more of this mooning about under some sort of fey spell for him. He'd unravel the charms and snap them in bits.

But, hang him, therein lay the problem. To figure out what damnable tricks Lightning was playing, Traveler would have to get close again. Close enough to touch, to lay his hands on the youth's skin and read the true nature of the magic he used.

And he'd be as able to do that as pet a rattling viper!

Calm yourself, now, Traveler ordered his churning thoughts. *Are you not a wizard still, despite turning your back on your magic-touched kin? Use your wits to solve this knotty problem.*

Very well. Traveler scowled at the wagon wheel, which had bruised his toe when he'd kicked at it, and put his mind to work. To be sure and certain, Lightning would never let Traveler get close as he needed. All blazing fire and sharp edges -- oh, there was no doubt where the youth had gotten his name -- Lightning would drive him off as soon as look at him.

Traveler began to smile. Well. There was a way around that, wasn't there?

With a thought, Traveler cloaked his physical appearance behind a mask of invisibility. Chancy, yes, to display such power, but he judged the use to be a risk worth taking. Anything to be free of Lightning's hold on him.

Handsome Lightning might be, and Traveler's cock might ache to plunder his tight, firm arse, but he wanted no strings binding him from one man to another. He'd have to be clever and cunning, but Traveler

Faire Grounds

had confidence in himself.

Seen by no man, woman or child, Traveler turned roundabout and crept back to Lightning's caravan.

This venture should work, but nothing was certain save for death and taxation. So they'd see what they'd see, wouldn't they?

* * *

Lightning didn't prove hard to find, busy as he still was snarling and pale with rage over the wreckage of his wares. The other Gypsies and folk of the road were giving him a wide berth -- familiar, no doubt, with Lightning's fire and his likely reaction to offers of help.

Traveler watched as Lightning slammed his final packet of goods into its chest. He inhaled, scenting the rich fragrance coming from those small cheesecloth squares. The aroma seemed vaguely familiar to him, and in a comforting way no less. Made him think of peace and quiet and treasured moments alone, of all things.

Lightning glared around himself, as if searching for any other intruders, but there were none but Gypsies and his Road-kin to be found. He still growled with anger as he climbed into his caravan and slammed the back gate behind him. Traveler suspected the youth would be dragging his pallet close to the edge, all the better to listen for sneaking thieves and guard his property.

But he'd seen the weariness on that young face, and Traveler knew Lightning would not be able to stave off sleep for much longer, not unless he was far more stubborn than Traveler could give him credit for.

Bah! Traveler snorted to himself. He should know better than to underestimate Lightning in anything. For all he knew, handsome Lightning would stay awake all the night through.

Didn't change the fact that Traveler had to get on the move with what he was doing. The longer he held the spell, the more chance he had of someone sensitive picking up on his power; the enchantment, too, was no easy thing to maintain, for he was out of practice in most magics.

Traveler shook his head as he gazed at Lightning's caravan. Witch-touched, to be sure, that such an old wagon should be in such fine condition. The wheels had such a balance that the cart barely rocked as Lightning moved to and fro.

If he had been such a man as were willing to dally with a handsome young lad for longer than needed to take his pleasure, Traveler knew he'd have hunted Lightning until the proud young man gave way. That tempting, he was, with his delicate face and stormy eyes and a mouth that might be innocent of all but angry words yet held so much potential for other, more pleasurable uses.

Time to get on with his work, and past time. Traveler lightened the weight of his body until he could float easily as a feather, and put one foot on the edge of Lightning's caravan.

He'd get to the bottom of this, and quickly.

Faire Grounds

* * *

Lightning frowned as he tugged his heavy bedding toward the back of the caravan, all the better to keep a watchful eye and ear out for his goods. The back of his neck itched as if someone were spying on him, despite being certain he'd been left well alone by Road-folk wary of his rage.

He hissed and swatted at his tingling nape. Insects? Perfect. All he needed. But if he put up protective screens, they'd hinder his way out to stop potential thieves.

Fine, then, he sulked. *I'll be eaten alive, but I don't care. No more loathsome Grounders will get their hands on my cargo if I have anything to say about the matter.*

Humphing, he jerked his pallet into place and glared at the innocent cot as if it were at fault for his current troubles. After a moment, he sighed. No use taking out his anger at the furniture, for the sake of the Lords. No use alienating the folk who would, by nature of their ties, be on his side.

Well and well, he'd make amends in the morning.

Just then, he had other things what needed doing.

Lightning moved further back into his caravan, going directly to a chest he hadn't seen open since Slipstream closed the lid shortly before his death from ague and a weakened heart. The thought of delving into the contents now nigh made him quail, but he summoned up his courage and thrust his chin out. If there were any better time to consult the Oracle-bones passed down from heir to heir, meant to guide them, he didn't know what would be.

The chest's hinges creaked in protest as Lightning levered the heavy lid open. Lords of the Road, he'd forgotten how many trinkets Slipstream had collected in his day. Books, too. Collections of tales, some he'd been forbidden to read due to his age -- hah, those might be worth a look later, eh?

But for the moment, Lightning had no problem locating the ancient leather bag he wanted. The pouch glowed as with foxfire, humming nigh silently as he reached to take it up. The prickle of being watched returned, giving Lightning cause to look around again in suspicion -- yet still, he saw neither soul nor shadow.

Foolish fancies, he chided himself. He'd business to attend to, uneasy as it made him. These Oracle-bones were no cheap trick. If they chose to speak, they'd tell their questioner exactly what they needed to know so long as the enchantment held. Not a thing to be consulted lightly, but faced with the dilemma of being soul-bound to a Deserter Gypsy, Lightning considered himself well in need of guidance.

Lightning headed for his pallet. He had an uncomfortable feeling that such an Oracle should be read in a more dignified position, but his muscles ached something fierce from a hard day's labors, and rather than betray his weakness he sank down onto the cot, on his stomach.

Lightning refused to give in to his nerves as he shook his pouch and then cast the old, yellow bones before him. They made no sense. He frowned, wondering if he should cast again.

But then --

A sound shivered through the caravan, as if someone or something was giving voice to a tremendous yawn.

Words echoed from the fallen bones, a voice Lightning realized was nowhere but in his own mind.

Who wakes me from my long sleep?

"It is the adopted son of Slipstream, called Lightning," he whispered, keeping his voice low enough not to be overheard. "I wake you in need of your advice."

The voice gave a rippling chuckle. Lightning shivered.

Ages come and go, but men are ever and always will be men. Well, what would you have of me, Lightning? The enchantments bound to me grow weak, but I have yet enough strength to speak with you.

"You know of the soul-binding, the one that ties the caretaker of these bones to his mate?"

Tcha. Of course I do. What other purpose do I serve but to guide these men? Waste not my time on questions worthy of a fool, and do not try my patience, youngling. Or not so young after all, are you? Nay, I can sense your age, and you're perilous near to twenty-

and-one. So close to the edge of the curse, and still alone?

"I have felt the touch of a man. I have seen my life-mate."

The bones chattered as if in irritation. **Then what purpose do I serve? Go to his side and take your pleasure. Let me conserve my energies for the one who comes after you.**

Lightning shook his head. "There is a problem. This man did not feel the same connection."

Are you sure? Think hard, and choose your words with care.

"I'm not thinking he sensed the pull," Lightning admitted. He should have known to be wholly honest with the bones. "After our eyes met, he didn't lay immediate claim as the stories tell, as my fathers swore would be. He passed me by."

Interesting. Unprecedented. Where is he now?

"I've no idea," Lightning said, exasperated. "He turns up when I least want him, and can be found neither here nor there when I'm in a mood to talk."

I cannot say I blame him. Fiery is your temper and sharp your words. Any man with a care to his skin would avoid you if they had a choice. Yet...this soul-mate should not be able to avoid you. The bones clacked one against the other, their movements seeming thoughtful. **I think you misjudge this man, young Lightning. You are far too quick to make snap decisions**

and let anger rule your heart, to say nothing of your actions. I am *certain* the enchantment still holds.

Lightning spoke quickly, lest the Oracle's wisdom abandon him altogether. "There is more. He's abandoned life on the road, though I know not why. He's a deserter. A traitor, my soul-mate? What sort of sense does such a thing make?"

So many new things. I understand how these may trouble you. But I also think you will have to ferret out most of the answers to your questions with your own wits, which are nothing close to dull. Be on your guard, as I feel sure is part and parcel of your nature, but do not build up thick walls against this soul-mate which he cannot overcome. How else will you complete the connection?

"I know I have no choice. It's late and late in my life for me to find a soul-mate, and I'm well aware I should be glad I've discovered him at last. Yet what he is and what I am...it is too much. Can the enchantments free me from this one and lead me to another?"

The Oracle bones jumped and popped where they had joints. **Foolish boy! There is no such trickery at my disposal or yours. This man is your mate; you must do the best you can.**

"I do not love him," Lightning whispered.

That is your affair. Leave me now. I have nothing more to say to you save this: bother me again only in dire peril. Lightning heard the sound of a sigh. **My task**

is completed.

"No -- no, wait!" His protest fell on deaf ears. The Oracle-bones' light faded. His counselor had gone.

Lightning slumped over his casting, heart wracked by despair. What was he to do now?

The ghostly touch at his back startled Lightning into a flinch. "Bones?" he queried, giving them a prod. "What goes?"

Lightning could *feel* enchantments filling his caravan. When he looked around, there was nothing to see, but he knew the touch of magic and could sense another man's presence at thirty yards.

Someone had slipped in, thinking to catch him off his guard.

"I know you're there," Lightning snapped. "You take your life in your hands, intruder. Begone before I -- I --"

Lightning felt, rather than heard, a rumble of laughter. Warm weight descended over his back, nothing he'd ever felt before but could swear was a man draping himself in comfort over Lightning's body.

"What are you doing?" Lightning "heard" inside his mind, a voice roughened and deepened as men did when they wanted to hide their identity.

"None of your affair." He gathered the Oracle-bones into their pouch with quick, tidy movements. "Have I not told you to be on your way?"

"Aye, but it amuses me to bide a while. And you cannot cast me out, Lightning. We have a score to settle, you and I."

"I've harmed no one at this faire. What do you think to claim from me?"

"Why, nothing but your obedience. That, and the truth. Who are you, Lightning? Who are you truly? A Gypsy who chanced to buy an enchanted caravan, or something more?"

"This caravan is mine by right, inherited from my fathers. And enchantments? Rubbish."

"Now, now. As if I would not know magic when it looked me in the eye, as would you. Your presence has haunted me since you entered these faire grounds, Lightning. What power do you hold to capture me thus and so?"

"I hold no power," Lightning lied. "I am but a Gypsy, as you see, and no threat to you."

"Unless you loose your sharp tongue on me. Already you have made several shallow cuts with that razor's edge. Tread lightly, I ask of you. And I inquire again: what sort of magic do you wield? I'll have the truth, if you please."

Lightning shaped his reply with care. "None that is not my own business, and mine alone."

"There is not a lie, but a diversion in what you say," the enchanted being mused in Lightning's mind. *"Perhaps a wicked youth such as yourself needs a lesson. Aye, I think a bit of schooling in manners would do you a world of good."* The weight on Lightning's back increased. He felt sure, now, that this was a male presence.

Despite his irritation and fear, Lightning could not help but hiss with pleasure. He'd seen other men do this, embracing their mates or lovers from behind, and now he knew why they liked the position so. There could be no mistaking the firm pressure of a hard cock pressing against the cleft of his arse -- nor the way that organ began to rub up and down, teasing him and knowing full well what effect he had on Lightning.

"I can taste your innocence. You have never known the intimate touch of a man, have you? Interesting. Someone of such beauty left unplundered at your age? Did you drive all suitors away with your cutting wit, or have they been too much in awe of your proud prettiness?

"Too personal a question," Lightning said through gritted teeth. The friction building up against his arse put him on edge, sending shocks of desire through his groin. He felt his cock begin to swell against the softness of the cot and ached to rub against it, but he'd not let on how this visitor affected him, no, not a bit.

The unseen man ran a finger down Lightning's back. Lightning automatically arched into the touch before biting his lip in dismay. Ach, this deception might not be one he could keep up for long.

Once soul-bound to another, none of Younger and Peddler's line were permitted to allow sex with another.

But then, none had ever wanted to break the taboo before now. The touch of his unseen visitor threatened to shatter Lightning's barriers, to make him want to toss caution heedless into blowing winds.

And then what would become of him?

"Stop," he breathed. "Please, stop." The words chafed at him, but Lightning knew no other recourse. "I cannot."

"Ah, but I think you can." Clever, inexorable hands drew Lightning's trews down, baring his arse to the cooling night air. *"I'll have what I want here, proud Gypsy. And you do not want to say me nay. Not really. Truth, now."*

Lightning shuddered. He half expected the Lords of the Road to descend on him in a storm of wrath, but this felt nigh worth the risk. He chanced damnation as he gave in and shook his head.

"Good lad," the voice crooned. *"Turn over for me now, Lightning. I can feel how desperately you want to rub yourself against this cot, and I would see the stiff branch that you have grown between your legs."*

Hands pressed at Lightning, guiding him over onto his back. His cock slapped against his lower belly, so swollen it was, dripping a thin, sticky stream against his skin. He felt shame -- no one had ever seen him thus before -- and also a thrill of excitement.

If he were on his road to damnation, then he would fly down instead of sinking like a stone. Yet he still marveled at his own daring as he reached down to stroke his prick, the organ pulsing in his grip. "So you see," he murmured. "What will you do with me now?"

"Appreciate a new side to you I have not seen before, and not only your body's position." The voice had a definite tinge of

amusement. And lust. Deep, heavy lust. Lightning caught a whiff of pure male essence, musky and thick, and inhaled deeply. So this was what it felt like to be with another man.

He had always wondered.

By the Road Lords, this was like unto walking in paradise.

"So tasty," his unseen visitor approved. *"I crave a taste, Lightning. I'll have that flavor on my tongue unless you push me away."*

Curious, Lightning reached for where he guessed his guest's shoulders would be, and encountered what felt like solid flesh. He had a moment where he nigh did shove the man back, but damn his own hide, he lacked the moral strength. Who could resist such a temptation?

"I'll take silence as your answer, then." The man gave a low laugh. *"This, I believe, I will enjoy. Ready yourself, for I come now."*

Lightning had but one startled second for the words to sink in, and then hot, tight wetness surrounded the head of his cock. He shouted in surprise as an eager tongue ran circles around his sensitive flesh, then again as the tip of that tongue jabbed into his seed-slit.

The suction drew back. *"So innocent, and so hungry for this. You'll come quickly, I vow, but we will meet again and take our time."*

"Yes," Lightning agreed, desperate for the mouth to return. "My word."

The voice exhaled in deep satisfaction -- and to Lightning's relieved pleasure, surrounded his cock again. Lightning felt soft lips slide up his shaft, engulfing him in his mystery man's scorching mouth, and then the bump of his cock against something hard.

He felt a powerful squeeze as throat muscles constricted around his prick, and nearly came.

"Wait," he gasped. "Please, wait -- I'll spend --" And Lords, he did *not* want this to be over so soon!

But he was given no choice. The invisible man swallowed again, dragging a deep groan from Lightning's gut, and then Lightning felt the barest scrape of teeth over his cock.

He arched off the bed as he shot his load of seed, thrashing and wailing fit to match a banshee. The man withdrew far enough to swallow every drop of Lightning's come, not a drop spilled. So odd, to see his own organ jerking in pleasure and his seed disappearing into nothingness, but so help him if Lightning felt like stopping to think.

The last of Lightning's thick fluid emptied from his balls and down his shaft. Lightning slumped back, all but boneless, his muscles relaxed to a state of total relaxation. He'd not have been able to move for all the wide world, had anyone demanded it of him at the moment. "So good," he panted. "So good."

Lightning felt the man's hands on his hips. *"Shall I turn you over once again, pretty Gypsy? I have not yet taken all the pleasure I would like. I'd have your arse, I would, pushing my cock into your cherry hole."*

Alarm sparked. What he had done was against the rules for sure and true, but if he were to surrender the whole of his virginity -- no, no, not to be dreamed of. "Don't,"

Lightning yelped. "I've sworn to remain pure for my soul-mate. I'm sullied enough already. No more, I beg."

"The denial of my urges is almost worth hearing your tongue shape itself around a plea." The man's weight withdrew. *"But as I have said, we will meet again, young Lightning. And perhaps you will not deny me when next we join."* Lightning felt the hungry press of lips against his neck, but even as he craned into the kiss, the man withdrew.

"You're leaving?" Lightning felt a twinge of fear.

"I will not go far, but yes, I leave you now. Bide you well, Lightning...and do not forget me."

Lightning laughed, the sound he'd almost forgotten bubbling from his throat. "As if I could."

"See that you do not."

And with a slight gust of wind, Lightning's visitor disappeared as if he had never been.

Lightning slumped against his cot, head all a-whirl. What had he done? This was forbidden, such a wrongness that no one in his line dared speak of such. Yet he'd felt more deeply touched by his mystery guest than he'd sensed from Traveler.

How? Why?

No answers came to mind.

But as he lolled upon his cot, his cock still exposed if now lying flaccid between his legs, Lightning heard a soft rapping on the back of his caravan. "Ho, the wagon," he was addressed in familiar tones. "Let me in, Lightning. We have much to discuss."

Lightning's heart sank and thumped erratically all at the once. He knew this visitor, and knew him well.

Traveler.

Chapter Four

Lords of the Road, but Lightning was a fair sight sprawled out on his back, legs parted brazenly, displaying the more than decent-sized cock on him. Not slim all over, was he?

But although the youth showed all the signs of just having had a fine, fine time -- *which I should know, for wasn't I there?* -- Traveler could see Lightning's customary irritation tightening his shoulders. The boy jerked at his trews, pulling them up to hide his tasty treat. "What in the hells are you doing here?" he snarled as he rolled over and up onto his knees. "What kind of meddling do you have in mind now, Traveler?"

Traveler chose his words with care. "There's been a great fuss between us two since you entered the faire grounds. Shouldn't be this way between two Gypsies, especially now as we've all got to pull together against the Grounders."

"You still call yourself a Gypsy? From the stories I hear, you've set down roots. No better than one of them."

Lords, lords, look at the fire in Lightning's face! "As you like, but I'm Gypsy to the bone. My reasons for settling after years on the

Road are my own."

Lightning eyed Traveler with suspicion. Traveler hid a sigh. He might be sweet enough when he let go of those prickles and took down his hair, but on his guard the lad were fiercer than his namesake.

"I've come to make peace, you thickheaded lunk," Traveler said with as much patience as he could muster. The insult slipped out on its own. "We need no fights among our own kind. One follows another's example, and soon there'll be clan after clan at one another's throats. For the sake of the road and all its travelers, I'm asking we declare a pax."

It was, more than like, the slur on his character which brought Lightning stiffly upright, blowing like an indignant horse. But if the youth had any sense -- and Traveler did not count him a dullard -- he'd see the wisdom being put forth.

"Very well." Lightning looked to be swallowing down hot words in favor of the clipped syllables that emerged. "Peace between us, Traveler, and a good night to you."

Well, now, this wouldn't do at all. Traveler had more investigating to do in Lightning's mysteriously enchanted wagon, and truth be told, despite his prickles Lightning had truly caught his fancy.

The feel of his thick, savory prick between my lips...bold, bold, taking what he wanted. Traveler had only intended a quick nose around, but the sight of Lightning laid out, trim arse ever so tempting, had driven him to his impromptu seduction.

The youth was worse than poppy-flower juice. One drop, and a man would do anything to get another.

"May I come in?" Traveler asked, trying to look harmless and amiable as he might. "Or will you come out?"

"Why should I permit the one or agree with the other?"

Prickles! Traveler kept his own irritation under wraps, a skill born of long practice. "So we can have a talk, man to man. Get all this worked well out, instead of depending on a few words to seal our peace."

Though if it were at all possible, he'd still have loved to turn Lightning over his knee. A good spanking, yes, that's what the brat needed.

The image of that honey-colored arse glowing red from slap after slap of Traveler's own hand made his cock give a twitch.
Perhaps if I can slip in under-my-cover again. Such a risk to use so much magic, but now he'd gotten the idea he found himself mightily tempted to try and see what happened.

He more than less suspected Lightning would enjoy being mastered. He'd put up a fight, then submit ever so sweetly.

Worth the magic, in Traveler's opinion.

He scowled at himself. So, he lusted after the youth. Done and done. He couldn't be forgetting his true purpose for visiting, though, could he? There was something about Lightning or his caravan that tingled with ancient enchantments, perhaps hooking him in a snare, and Traveler would have no part of any such.

As he'd been thinking, Lightning had followed suit. "I'll not let you in," Lightning said abruptly. "But I'll come out. Better that the other folk see us coming to good terms, seeing as you're concerned about our ire spreading."

Wise. Traveler approved. However, that meant he'd have to canoodle his way back in the caravan again, damn fool he was for getting distracted by Lightning's tight young body instead of snooping as had been the plan.

Lightning was just too much for a man of Traveler's natural-born lustiness to resist. Case in point, he couldn't help admiring the lean strength in Lightning's legs as he climbed gracefully over the backboard of his caravan and made the short jump with ease, landing on his bare toes.

He turned to look up at Traveler. A good distance up, as for all Lightning's wrath, Nature had contained it in a small package. Traveler suspected how Lightning, as most slight men felt, wouldn't be inclined to show any quarter against a bigger fellow. He'd be ever more on his guard with Traveler looming over him.

So, Traveler sat, loose and easy, not a bit of a threat in the way he went down and neatly tucked his feet beneath him. He knew this to be foolishness and pure vanity, but he'd used a bit more of the magic to tidy himself up. Dangerous, but well and well, it were a simple enough spell and common at that for Grounders and Road-folk alike to purchase for occasions when they'd no time to pull themselves together.

And so he appeared before Lightning in the clothing he preferred, sturdy trews made of doeskin suede in natural rich brown, and a thickly woven tunic made of good sturdy wool, flecked green and brown, well fit to keep out the chill from the winds on the sea. Casual enough to show his intentions were merely friendly, tidily formal enough to let Lightning know he took this serious-like.

Damn his hide, though, when he'd called the magic he'd washed himself clean of sweat and smoothed his hair into the bargain. *What are you after, Traveler, hoping to impress this lad with your good looks?* he jeered at himself.

Lightning examined Traveler as he, too, sat down. His own outfit bore more than a few stains from a long day's labors, but he dared Traveler with a spark of his eyes to say one word about his state of dishevelment.

Traveler pretended to take no notice as he proceeded to the next step of making peace: a sharing of salt and bread. Well and well, he might have made the offer anyway. Lightning looked to be the type who was forever hungry, and Traveler could hear the rumbling in the youth's stomach. "The hour's late. Would you take a bite and sup with me?"

Natural wariness warred with good manners. *Someone* had taught Lightning well, though no doubt, they had despaired of him a time or three. "Food would be welcome," he said stiffly. "I'll share a meal with you, as you request."

"Good!" Traveler's magic could extend so

far as to create provender from thin air, if he liked, but that took a fair bit of time. He could have swiped a portion from someone else's stores, but he'd not have stolen from any of the families roundabout. Gypsies, even deserters like him, did *not* thieve.

And so he raised one hand and waved to a nearby fire, cheerily calling: "Ho to you, Heartsease!"

A plump woman standing guard over a heavy iron stew pot, swatting away swarming younglings with a solid iron ladle, looked up and shaded her eyes for a better view. "Ah, so it's you," she said, not unkindly. "What do you call me for?"

"A trade, if it pleases you. A purchase. The food you cook smells wonderful, and I find myself with a craving for a taste. I've a bit of coin to pay you."

"Hmm. A copper for a pot of stew; aye, that would please me well enough."

"If you'll pardon me?" Traveler asked. Lightning narrowed his eyes, but nodded.

Traveler felt Lightning's gaze tingling on his skin all the way over to Heartsease's cooking fire. Tingling just like the magics clinging to the youth and his caravan. *Intriguing.*

He bowed courteously to Heartsease. There were some who wouldn't give him the time of day, being deserter and all, but those were few enough in number and Heartsease was a soundly practical woman besides. She knew to cook enough for her vast brood and some over for guests who were always drawn close by the savory scents of what she had in her stew pot.

"Mannerly, mannerly," she scoffed, although Traveler could tell from her light blush that Heartsease was well pleased. "Well, then. Our bargain?"

"I've no kettle to carry the meal in," Traveler apologized, "but I'll add an extra copper for the loan of a container."

Heartsease thumped him with her ladle. "As if I'd grudge you the loan of a carrier. One of you bunch, go and find a big deep bowl for me," she ordered the gaggle of children. "Hop to, now!"

One of the giggling lot, probably hoping he'd earn an extra portion, scrambled to the open wagon and quickly found what had been called for. He brought it to his mother with a gap-toothed smile. "Will this do?"

"Good enough." Heartsease's face softened as she tousled the boy's sleek hair. "Now, Traveler. Take the bowl and hold it out for me. Careful, now, this will be hot."

Traveler obeyed meekly as a doe, careful with the balance as Heartsease dipped her ladle into the large cooking pot and loaded his bowl. She proved generous as reputation painted her, giving him portion after portion of rich broth and boiled shellfish and sliced tubers, then sprinkled red pepper over the lot.

"There. Will this satisfy?"

"More than." She'd offered more food than he and Lightning could eat together, but the amount was fair worth for the coin he'd offered earlier. "You're a good woman, Heartsease, so you are."

"Bah. Save your pretty talk for those who'll appreciate such." Her look turned sly. "Those who you appreciate, yourself, which I know full well isn't my sort of creature." She tilted her head at Lightning despite his rude, blunt stare at them. "A pretty one, isn't he? Ah, but he's more of a devil in him than any of these younglings. What do you plan to do with him, Traveler?"

Traveler gave her an honest answer. "Right now I've nary a clue, Heartsease. But I suspect you'll find a way to satisfy your curiosity by and by." He darted in to kiss her cheek, sending her spluttering and red-faced with feigned indignation. "My thanks for the meal."

Chuckling to himself, Traveler wheeled about -- carefully -- to make his way back to Lightning's caravan. He set the bowl down before his lad and sat down, cautious not to jostle the steaming stew nor lose a single drop.

"I've provided my share," he said jovially. His statement contained a hidden hint. Lightning must needs add to the meal as his part of the peace-making. Traveler did hate to ask, as he suspected Lightning's leanness was born of frequent hunger. But ah, he'd leave the leftover stew for Lightning to satisfy his stomach with another time.

Lightning crackled at Traveler, but gave him a stiff nod. "One moment."

Traveler admired Lightning's backside as he climbed into his caravan. Heart-shaped, well-toned, positively perfect. Road Lords, but a single look at the youth made Traveler want to forget all else in the hopes of seducing those tight trews right off Lightning's arse -- again.

Not through trickery, though. For sure, he had behaved shamefully to attack Lightning when he couldn't be seen. Lightning might have succumbed before, under cover, but he'd never have let Traveler near his body in such a manner had he known truly who was taking their pleasure with him.

Traveler swallowed a sigh, but did shake his head in frustration. Why did he *care?* Making peace was one thing; a display of pax was indeed something other Gypsies needed to see. So help him, though, if this wasn't more than mere form. He *wanted* Lightning's forgiveness, and the settling of their ill will.

Lightning had somehow come to matter to Traveler, and he didn't like this, no, not one bit.

Speaking of whom, Lightning leapt down from his caravan with the same supple grace as he'd displayed before. He carried a make-shift parcel of food bound in a kerchief, which he dropped beside the stew, and --

"Spoons?" Traveler asked curiously, glancing at the wooden utensils.

The faintest of grins tugged at Lightning's lips. "You forgot them."

Traveler all but laughed aloud. So the boy had a sense of humor, and the joke was truly on him, wasn't it? "So I did," he agreed with good cheer. "What have you brought to our table?"

Perhaps regretting his brief lapse, Lightning mutely opened his kerchief to reveal a half-loaf of bread, not fresh but not too old, two apples, and a wedge of sharp-scented cheese. "I've no ale," he said, clipped. "And I've not had a chance to go for fresh water, if they've allowed our kind access to such."

"Never mind the drinks; this is good enough for peace accord." Traveler picked up an apple, polished the fruit on his sleeve, and took a crunching bite. Sweet juice flowed over his tongue as he savored the mealy flesh.

Lightning pursed his lips, then picked up the cheese and broke off a morsel to pop between his tempting lips.

Traveler could easily think of something *else* he'd like to see swallowed by that mouth...

"Ware," Lightning said, looking up with uncanny speed. "Birds abovehead." Traveler heard the rough *caw, caw, caw* of a crow.

Oh, blast.

Ravens were the worst of bad omens for the Gypsies. For one of their breed to attend this meeting boded ill if Lightning were the superstitious type. Not thinking, Traveler grasped Lightning's trim wrist. "Pay no heed. 'Tis only a bird, not a sign or a warning."

Lightning jerked away. He said nothing, but his crackling shield toughened. Either he'd objected to the touch, or he did believe in signs. Either way, they were one step forward and two steps back again.

Traveler exhaled a deep breath. He was going to get nowhere with this youth, that much was clear. He dipped his wooden spoon into the bowl of stew, unable to stop a hum of pleasure at the rich, salty taste, and waited for Lightning to do the same.

The way Lightning's eyes widened when he tasted the fresh, flavorful stew sent a twinge through Traveler's heart. Lords, but this one needed somebody to take care of him. See him fed properly, reinforce his manners, and love him hard enough to sleep sound at night.

What had possessed him, though, that *he* wanted to be the one to take charge of fractious Lightning?

"Mew?"

Traveler glanced down in surprise to see a small, dainty tiger-striped cat arranged neatly at his feet. "Mew," she voiced again, sounding firm.

"Patpaw, leave him be," Lightning scolded. Then, he blushed. Traveler hid a smile at Lightning's embarrassment over the cat's name. No doubt he didn't like showing his softer side. Yet the cat's existence was proof enough such a thing existed, wasn't it? Patpaw looked healthy and well-fed, sleekly groomed and bursting with self-confidence.

"She's a lovely lady," Traveler ventured, letting the cat sniff his fingers. She approved, bumping her head against his hand. *Where had she been hiding before, when I was -- we were -- well, she's a sneaky puss, then, too.*

"Bah." Lightning crossed both arms over his chest. "She jumped on board while I bartered in a village off the road, and wouldn't be cast aside."

"A taste of company on the road does no harm to any man." Speaking of which...which clan did Lightning belong to? Had he chosen to travel alone, or had they cast him out?

Faire Grounds

The mystery deepens.

Lightning shrugged. "Patpaw, you've eaten once tonight. Get your nose away from our stew."

Patpaw hissed. Lightning glared her down. She grumbled, but then, casual as if she didn't care, tripped lightly away and vaulted easily into the caravan, clearly well at home.

"I've a cat of my own," Traveler said casually. "A burly black Tom twice the size of your Patpaw, for I've not the knack of keeping him from extra snacks when he can steal a bite or three." He relaxed into his tale, glad to have someone who might listen. Cats, too, were considered terrible bad luck for folk of the road, no matter how useful they were for keeping mice away from precious goods. He'd never understood why Gypsies feared them. Interesting that Lightning should own one. "A couple of years back, someone set a sack of kittens afloat in the sea. I spotted the bag, but I could only save the one. He's a good companion, though. Suits my nature and knows my ways."

"And what would those ways be, deserter?" Lightning snapped, as if the question had been bubbling below his surface. Ah, another reason for Lightning to despise him, aye? "You make so free with your tales and your other speeches. Tell me this: what takes a Gypsy off the road and plants him in one spot just like one of these bedamned Grounders?"

Traveler took a deep breath to answer, but before any words could leave his mouth, he winced at a sudden, burning pain above his breastbones. One of the wizard's trinkets he dared not do without, the small chunk of pure crystal dangling on a cord around his neck was meant to warn him when another of his magic-kin had a message to pass on. Curses on their timing!

Lightning's sharp eyes missed nothing. "Something pains you?"

"Nothing," Traveler reassured him, manfully holding back another wince as the crystal flared against his skin. Such heat was like to set his wool afire, and wouldn't he have a time explaining himself then?

Blast. He'd have to save examining Lightning's wagon for another time.

Traveler levered himself up off the ground. He did *not* offer Lightning a hand, letting the youth follow suit on his own. "We've made our peace, then?" he asked, formal-like. "No more trouble between us?"

"Not so long as we stay out of one another's way."

Traveler prickled with irritation. Welladay, he'd hardly be able to find out what he needed to know if he stayed clear of Lightning, would he? "I'd rather we sought to become friends," he offered. "Mayhap we'll meet again and share another meal."

"Don't count your chickens." Lightning's gaze had gone shuttered. "Good-night, then."

He deliberately turned his back on Traveler and climbed up into the caravan, leaving him with the mess of food to tidy, his insult clear. Pax, bah! Apparently Lightning would go through the form, but substance was another

Faire Grounds

matter.

Traveler rubbed the bridge of his nose, feeling a headache born of tension form. Lords of the Road, this Gypsy youth and his attendant mysteries would be the death of a simple wizard who wanted nothing more than to be left alone. He scowled at the caravan, itching to take control and demand the answers he sought, as well as giving Lightning a good hard shake into the bargain.

Tempting as the notion might sound, though, it wouldn't do. He'd have to be patient.

This did *not* please him.

Nor did the heat of the messenger crystal, nigh scorching a hole through his flesh. This wouldn't wait 'till he reached his island.

Damned if he'd show such poor courtesy as Lightning, though. Traveler made well and sure to secure the foodstuffs, even wiping their spoons off on the kerchief, before he walked away at a careless pace meant to draw no attention. He kept up the pretense until he made his way down to the shore, and found a good stone cranny, one of those that had given Mossy Rock its name, to hide behind.

Gritting his teeth with proper annoyance, Traveler pulled out the crystal. It pulsed reprovingly at him, as if the speaker had grown well and truly impatient in their wait. He licked the pendant -- blood would be better, but any fluid of the body would do in a pinch -- and whispered, "Here I am. What do you need?"

"Janos?" a tinny, disembodied voice demanded.

"Traveler."

"Janos," the voice corrected. "This is Nikolai. Have you a few minutes to spare for once?"

Traveler growled with frustration. He despised the use of his other name, and if any Gypsy were to hear him being addressed thus...bad enough he'd gone deserter.

If they knew him to be a true Grounder, not a Gypsy at all, his life among the people he loved would be over sure as sunrise.

"Call me Traveler, or I end our discussion at once."

Nikolai snorted. "Traveler. Ridiculous conceit. No one's seen through your disguise yet?"

"And never will, if I have my way. Now have at it. What's so urgent you use the crystal to get my attention?"

"Humph. Jan -- Traveler, I've had contact from the castle today, a visitor asking a few too many questions. I thought you should know."

"Who came? What did they ask?" Traveler demanded, his full attention immediately fixed on the crystal.

"They wanted you to come home and take your place as heir before your brother is the ruination of them all," Nikolai said simply. "And it could happen, as I've told you several times before. The family needs you among them. As for the dangers, you could hire guards and bravos to watch your back, and live safely enough; richly, too, as befits a man of your station."

"Never." Traveler had made his choice, for reasons that remained good, and he wouldn't be changing his mind now. "I walk my own path now."

"Oh, yes, living your dreams while Andrei squanders the family fortunes and alienates all our allies with his ranting. The man's mad, Traveler."

"Mad enough to destroy himself in the bargain. When you last pestered me, you made me aware of Andrei's tastes for absinthe and opium. He'll be dead within a year or so, and then the cousins can squabble amongst themselves for the leavings. This concerns me not."

"Will you break an old Steward's heart, then?"

Traveler burst into laughter. "Don't be after trying to play-act with me, Nikka. Leave well enough alone and let Andrei bring himself to his inevitable end. And leave me in peace. Lords of the Road, I should never have taught you this speaking-trick. I'd thought you a wizard summoning me."

"Would that I could find a decent wizard," Nikolai grumbled. "We could use one of those around here, too."

"Aye, but you know how my feelings lie in that quarter as well. Nikka, I've put my trust in you not to betray where I've gone to ground. You still deserve that trust, don't you?"

"As if I'd dare betray you. What was it you threatened me with? Red-hot chairs and blocks of ice at my feet? Your secret's safe enough with me, Janos. Traveler. Although I will have you know you're missed keenly as a son of my own breeding."

Traveler sighed. "As I miss you. But we are agreed -- this is for the best. Keep me apprised of any complications, but keep this enchantment for last resorts," he warned. "Fare you well, Nikka."

"Have it your way, then, as ever you have. Fare you well, Traveler."

The crystal went dark.

Traveler curled his fist around the speaking-rock, squeezing tight, and began to rock to and fro in deep disturbance.

From worse to worse. I shudder to think -- what will happen next?

* * *

Lightning tossed on the pallet where he'd taken such pleasure earlier, unable to get comfortable -- perhaps from the memories all-attendant when he lay himself down, aye?

Lords of the Road, what was wrong with him? This had been the perfect opportunity to be open with he whom the enchantments declared to be his soul-mate. Yet his shame at what he'd almost been caught doing had put him right on the edge, and his temper had refused to cool enough to be more than barely civil.

I'll never get the problem solved at this rate. Lightning thumped his pillow. He'd been warned about the sorts of trouble his fiery nature would get him into.

He recalled what Slipstream had said once:

Faire Grounds

"Lad, if I knew no better, I'd swear you are born of a union between thunder and your namesake lightning. What's in you that causes you to act this way? Care, my son, have a care. Someday you'll need patience more than food -- but will you have learned by then?" He'd stroked Lightning's hair with one frail old hand. "I wish I understood you better, boy. I wish you understood yourself."

Lightning closed his eyes tightly. Very well; he'd swallow his pride and try again, this time humble as he could make himself be. He doubted, though, he could press Traveler much further. Any man who *was* a man should despise him after being so insulted and slighted.

Yet there remained the tie between them, and the curse looming ever heavier over his shoulder.

He frowned in sudden thought. Perhaps there was a way to gain Traveler's good graces, should they have run out. Notions tumbled into his head, forming themselves into a rough plan, a plan he'd put into action on the morrow.

Yes, there might just be a way...

Chapter Five

Mirrors, ah, those were dangerous things for a Gypsy to carry in his wagon. Too easily broken -- bad luck -- and those you didn't want prying in your personal business could use them all too easily as a way of taking a look around -- worse luck still -- and they led to vanity -- which Horsetail had snorted about as worst of all.

For all that, though, as Lightning prepared

himself in the dim morning light to go and seek out Traveler, he did wish he had something to check his reflection in.

He'd slept lightly and ill the night before, dreaming of phantom mouths swallowing his swollen prick, driving him to distraction with a talented tongue, aching to feel the same again. When he'd risen, it had been to sticky sheets and relief to spy the first glimmer of dawn in the sky.

There was no time in a Gypsy's life but the present, and no sense in wasting the day. Lightning would have to make ready for what he planned. He huffed a bit over the thought of currying favor, but Slipstream's advice had always been to present one's best appearance to those from whom you sought approval.

Well, not so much approval, nay. More like the need to make amends -- and to have his questions answered, as well, no matter how he might be galled at supplicating himself for any cause or reason.

Blast his temper, anyway. Lightning gritted his strong white teeth and shoved any lingering irritation aside. The emotions would serve him ill on the errand he'd determined to pursue.

And so, mindful of Slipstream's advice, Lightning's first task had been to seek out the source of fresh water Gypsies used. He'd been surprised and pleased to find not only a stream from which they could drink, but a blocked-off pool where one might bathe. Ah, but he'd been glad to rid himself of the travel grime and the sweat he'd worked up when... when...

There he went, blushing like a girl again.

Safe in his wagon, Lightning could shake his head and click his tongue at his foolishness. Had he gone mad the afternoon before? He'd let a stranger all a-cloaked with invisibility into his caravan and been wanton as a half-copper whore. He, who'd vowed to hold his virginity safe for his life-mate.

Although he supposed, dubiously, he hadn't *quite* broken the taboo. He'd stopped his visitor before the man's cock invaded his arse. But he'd drawn quite close enough to lines that oughtn't be crossed, for certain sure.

Madness -- or magic. Both choices made Lightning shiver. He depended on the lingering enchantments of Younger and Peddler, but strange magics posed a potentially dreadful threat. Madness... perhaps the greater of two evils.

Was it insanity, mayhap, which made him think Traveler to be his soul-mate?

It didn't feel like he'd lost his mind. Lightning poked and prodded at his inner thoughts until he felt satisfied of his rightful senses -- a relief, to be sure. *Although,* he thought with a hackling of his shoulders, *what I propose to do is sheer lunacy. Yet what choice do I have?* He had to settle the question about Traveler's tie to him.

And to do that, he must seek out Traveler himself.

Lightning dug out and opened a trunk once the property of Slipstream, full of fine clothes no respectable peddler should own. Bright with Gypsy color and fanciful embroidery despite being centuries out of date, the fabric remained good and solid and would suit him well.

Legend held it these were the garments Peddler had made a gift of to Younger as part of their joining. Indeed, they felt enchanted.

All the better, then, to garb himself in such as he went to seek the truth of his fate.

Stripping down wholly bare, careless of his nudity in the privacy of the caravan, Lightning considered his choices. Which color would best compliment his skin? What would make him a more appealing morsel?

He stopped himself in disgust. By the Road Lords, he could only bend his pride so far. Snatching up the first shirt and trews at hand, he slammed the trunk and robed himself in scarlet tunic with golden trimming and tight black trews with silver lacings. The whole of the ensemble fit him like a glove, as if they'd been tailored to his exact fit.

Familiar enchantments, the sort he'd grown used to, but they rattled Lightning's nerves all the same.

He undid his hair from its rumpled braid, tsking as the heavy strands fell in loose tangles down past his knees, and plucked up a sturdy comb from his grooming kit. Getting the bone teeth through his snarled locks was a time-consuming job, but Lightning refused to give up until each hank had been tamed into a silky-smooth waterfall.

Despite warnings against vanity, Lightning indulged himself in a moment of admiration. He knew of no one who had hair like his, so sleek and black enough to have blue highlights. Lucky hair, and the mark of one whose Gypsy

Faire Grounds

blood ran thick and deep.

Almost felt a shame to bind his tresses up in a braid again, but pfah! Loose hair was only good to look at, not practical at all for a vagabond's life, nor for his chosen task. He bound his hair smoothly with a practiced touch, felt to make sure he'd done the task right, and called the job well done, as it needed to be.

Dressed and combed, he should have been ready. Something felt lacking, though. Lightning stood with fists on his hips, raking his memories for what he might have missed -- then turned pink at a thought which suggested itself.

He dared not.

Or did he?

What worry was there over misinterpretation of his intentions when he planned to present himself to the man he felt uncannily drawn to?

He'd do this, then. With a resigned snort, Lightning bent to the small furnace bolted to the floor of his caravan and used the ash-shovel to fetch out some soot. He then searched and found among his wares a small quill pen, and touched its tip lightly to the coal dust.

This he *did* need a looking-glass for. Lightning searched roundabout until he found a copper pan meant for trade, and propped the thing up to peer at his wavery reflection. Ever so carefully, he used the quill and soot to line his eyes. The effect startled him, turning already dark and luminous eyes to those of a seductive rogue.

Again he wondered: was this the wisest choice?

Ah, bah. Lightning stowed his supplies and thrust out his chin. What was done was done, and he'd not back down now.

And now he felt ready.

Will Traveler take pleasure in what he sees? Will he know what I have in mind? Lightning blushed again in embarrassment and scowled down at his traitorous cock, which seemed to take a great interest in winning Traveler's approval.

Behave, he ordered the determined organ. *None of your funny business until or unless I've satisfied my curiosity.*

Head held high, Lightning climbed out of his caravan to set light foot on the soft sedge grass. Now, who was the woman Traveler had purchased their meal from the night before? Ah, there she stood, staring at him in curiosity and shock, as well he supposed she should at a Gypsy dressed in such out-of-date peacock feathers.

He approached the dame humbly, as befit her greater years. "Road-kin and Gypsy mother, if it please you, I would beg a favor."

Heartsease -- was that her name? -- Lightning couldn't remember for sure -- blinked out of her startled examination of his face and finery to address him as one Road-rider to another. "Well and well. I'd thought you too proud to request a thing," she said, not unkindly. "What do you seek?"

"My goods. I do not fear Grounders, but I

suspect some of their ilk may try to slip in under cover of disguise."

"I'd not put it past them. But for shame, that you should have to ask," Heartsease reproved. "Unless they come armed with enchantments, and we're left all unaware -- as happened before, though we'll keep a closer watch now to be sure -- I and the rest of our clans will take on the protection of your precious cargo." She paused. "Although, to satisfy an elder's curiosity, what lies in those packets you guard so fierce?"

Could he trust her? Ah, but he'd have to, wouldn't he? "Tea," Lightning replied, clipping the word short.

Her eyes widened. "And so much of it. I never! No wonder you're wanting to keep such valuables safe. We'll take special care, then -- but once word gets out, you'll have Gypsy-kin wheedling samples from you. 'Tis our way, to share and share alike. You know this, aye?"

Lightning nodded. "I do." He'd just have to deal with the consequences when they came his way. The next sentence stuck in his throat on a knot of pride, but he choked it down. "Would you know where I might find Traveler this morning?"

Heartsease's face creased with open amusement. "Oh, ho, so that's the way of things, is it?" She chuckled. "You'll not find him on these shores. Last anyone spotted Traveler, he was making his way down to the sea. He'll have gone back to his island. He never stays long when he visits Mossy Rock."

Damn him. To chase so far after the man

would betray far more eagerness than Lightning was comfortable with.

He'd not hesitate now, though.

"And would you know where I might rent or borrow a boat?"

* * *

For all that Gypsies savored life, the beauty of the day went lost on Lightning as he unsteadily navigated the small fishing boat he'd humbled himself to rent from a Grounder, who'd looked at Lightning as if he suspected full well he'd never see his craft again.

Lightning wrinkled his nose. Full well he'd give this tub back, and that gladly. The interior looked none too clean, and the whole of the boat stank of dead fish.

Perfect. I'll greet Traveler with the fragrance of rotting mackerel.

He jumped and swore as the current threatened to sweep away one of his oars. Lords of the Road, he hadn't been afloat since he was barely old enough to look over the side, and then there had been Slipstream to steady him and Horsetail to man the paddles, his strokes strong and sure.

Traveler's claimed island, which he'd heard named "Starling" and called "cursed", lay directly in Lightning's sights. A chunk of uninhabitable-looking rock jutting out of the sea, it was. Lightning frowned, curious. If a Gypsy did turn deserter and go to ground, why pick such a hostile home?

Mystery upon mystery. How did one even

find a decent spot to row himself ashore?

The question was soon answered as Lightning drew closer. He spied a narrow gap between two of the fiercest-looking guardian rocks. Navigating his clumsy way through was no lark, but sheer determination guided him through at last.

Once past the obstacles, Lightning pulled his boat to a stop and blinked in surprise. The dangerous rocks, it would seem, were merely a guardian ring around... this.

Welladay. Traveler liked his surprises, didn't he?

The true island lay peacefully within its ring of rocks, a gentle tide washing easy waves upon a sandy shore. Green, green grass grew thick and lush on smoothly rounded banks, along with fruit trees and, were he not mistaken, signs of a garden in ripe growth.

But in the middle -- well, there lay the greatest shock.

How he'd gotten the building materials was a puzzle to Lightning, but Traveler had built himself a proper home of wood and stone. Rounded as were houses often seen in lands far distant, with a dome for a roof, it looked trim as any caravan and had been painted in gloriously bright Gypsy colors. Only a low, rocky wall served to keep out any who might -- and Lightning doubted there'd be many, if *any* -- mean to visit.

Lightning could not help but stare as he drew his boat ashore. Still clumsy, he managed to wet the calves of his trews as he stumbled out, splashing in shallow water.

Now I'll look like Patpaw after a bath, he groused. *But I won't turn back. I won't. I won't.*

He made his way up the banks with his jaw set stubbornly, all the way to the guardian wall, where he was forced to stop in puzzlement. There seemed to be no gate he could spy, and climbing over struck him as rude. Rude wouldn't start them off on the foot Lightning hoped for.

Blessed be. What now?

"Rrrowl!"

Lightning startled as, from seemingly nowhere, a black cat of amazing size sprang up on top of the wall. He settled down on his haunches and examined Lightning with the cool detachment and eerie sense of knowing only a cat could muster. His tail twitched -- though in uncertainty or threat -- Lightning could not tell.

He did as Traveler had the night before with Patpaw, extending his fingers for this beastie to smell. "I'm meaning you no harm," he crooned as he did with his own cat in a rare tender moment when she curled against him and purred. "I've come a-visiting to meet your master, no more."

The cat tilted its head. Lightning shuddered, feeling strange magic raking his body head to toe.

To his relief, the vast animal began to purr. He licked at Lightning's hand with a rough tongue. Nimble in his navigation, the cat turned his back and glanced over his shoulder, then hopped down.

Lightning supposed it could be construed as

Faire Grounds

an invitation to follow suit. And what other choice did he have?

The wall was low enough for an easy vault, but Lightning nigh regretted the jump once he landed inside. More of the magic washed over him, a curious presence seeking and searching the corners of his heart and soul he'd much prefer remain hidden.

"Leave off," he said firmly, hands going to his hips. "I've said I mean no harm, and there's a Gypsy's word. Stop your searching and let me go on my way."

The entities withdrew in obedience. Lightning breathed a bit easier as they left and took stock of himself to see if any lasting influence lingered.

None he could tell. Good.

Pulling himself upright, Lightning tested his voice's ability to give a strange call. "Ho, the Gypsy-house!" he greeted. "Ho, Traveler! Be you in your home?"

* * *

Now wasn't this interesting? Traveler had his window mage-guarded so anyone looking in could not see him looking out, so he got the chance to drink his fill of the proud young Lightning, of all folk, waiting on his lawn.

The lad's got balls, and brass ones at that, daring to find his way to my homestead. What does the pestersome boy want now, to insult me on my own grounds?

Still... I saw Luck giving his approval, and that does count for something.

Besides, Traveler's curiosity had been roused.

Curiosity, and cock.

The selfsame organ rose and swelled at the sight of Lightning. Had he decorated his eyes with coal? By damn, he had. Eyes a queen would envy looked even wider and brighter than they had before, giving him an air of seduction mixed with odd innocence such as would wilt any man's self-control.

Road Lords, did Lightning even realize what a tasty morsel he looked? Even dressed in travel-stained workaday garb, his hair awry, he had stolen Traveler's breath. Now, dressed in fine fabrics, neat as one could be after sailing windy seas, he looked good enough to eat.

Which Traveler already knew, having tasted the youth's cock to his satisfaction the day before.

Would he let Lightning in? Aye, he would. But in a moment; let him wait a bit. Traveler wanted to capture the sight of this devastating Gypsy standing on his personal ground.

Not many knew this, and he kept the secret carefully guarded, but one of the magical arts Traveler had learnt was Art itself. Paintings, sculptures, even colored glass-work -- he could do them all if he had the right tools.

All he had immediately to hand, though, was a stick of soft lead and a rough-edged sheet of parchment, with which he'd thought to write down his tangled thoughts about Lightning in the hopes of uncovering solutions to his riddles.

How much better use, he decided, than to

capture the lad in a sketch instead?

The old skill came back easy as breathing, so it did, soft lines flowing from the lead onto Traveler's paper. The drawing took shape at a rapid pace, capturing every nuance of Lightning from his haughty stance to the glow in his eyes to the enticing, lean lines of his body.

Ah, but Traveler ached to unwrap those elegant clothes and see the youth laid out bare before him. The pressure in his cock and balls drew nigh unbearable, so enticed he grew.

Only when the sketch had been completed, and Lightning started to shuffle as if he doubted Traveler would answer his summons did Traveler put his paper aside and make for the front door.

He threw it open wide. "Ho, Lightning," he replied, calm despite his raging need to fuck the lad deaf and dumb. "What business brings you here?"

The blunt question took Lightning aback. No doubt he'd expected a courteous dance around the point, as Gypsies were wont to do. He blinked, giving Traveler to notice the thick black lashes over his amazing eyes, and blurted out: "What do you call the cat?"

A curious opening gambit. "His name is Luck."

Lightning laughed for no reason Traveler could fathom -- laughter! The merrily rippling sound stole Traveler's desire to seek the cause. Lightning's pleasure fueled his own, growing by the moment.

How much softer fiery Lightning seemed.

Why?

No less brash, though. The youth flicked a glance around Traveler's home. "You find great pleasure in your dwelling, aye?" He sounded curious, of a certainty wondering at Traveler's Desertion combined with how he had blended Gypsy design into his home.

"I love this place," Traveler replied, and let his statement rest.

The words drew a frown to Lightning's face. "Love," he repeated, scornful now. "What is love worth? There's only fate and, well, luck that brings fortune men can enjoy, but not very often *love*, as they claim."

"You have little belief in love, then?"

Lightning tossed his head. "I have only seen love once, between my fathers. As for the rest of the world, it is as I have said."

"Do you believe in lust, then? In passion?"

"Those are real enough, or so I have seen often and oft." Lightning narrowed his eyes. "Why do you ask?"

Traveler shrugged. Careful, even out on his warded rocky home, he extended a tendril of magic to read the Gypsy lad's heart. Ah, he did not tell the precise truth. Lightning had seen love before, and believed in its power -- but he did not expect any to come his own way.

More provocative still.

Impulsively, Traveler stood aside from his doorway. "Will you come in?" he offered. "I could fetch us water to drink, or a bite to eat, if you're hungered. I have plenty and to spare."

"No." Lightning drew himself up. "But I will enter, as you wish."

As if he's a king granting a commoner the favor of his presence. And why am I letting him past my barriers? Did the enchantment he'd felt -- and still did -- override his common sense?

More like it would be his hunger for Lightning's mouthwatering body.

"Into my chamber, said the spider to the fly?" Lightning queried with a taste of his familiar bite as he passed Traveler and made his way inside.

"Much better," Traveler grinned, urging Lightning on.

Lightning gazed at him in frank appraisal. "You are a puzzle to me, Traveler. I've come for my own reasons, but why would you invite me into your home?"

To lead you to my bed, and do as I will with your supple flesh and tight young arse.

Traveler cleared his throat. "Courtesy," he shrugged. "We'll let the biting insects in if we bide in the entryway much longer."

Lightning nibbled at his lip, a charmingly naive look for him. He firmed his shoulders in determination. "Aye, I'll enter. But leave the latch open."

Fair enough. Traveler did as he'd been bidden, then stepped back to consider his options. He might invite Lightning into his kitchen for a drink and plain speech, yet he had the oddest urge to let the youth in elsewhere. A room no one save himself had ever visited.

He'd be a fool to let Lightning get a glimpse.

Damned if he could master his urge despite knowing better. "Come with me," he invited. "I've something to show you I'll wager you've never seen the like of before."

Lightning's expression grew wary, but he nodded just the same. Strangely giddy despite the risk he took, Traveler led the way through the common room and to a case of books and shells mounted against the far wall. Too quick for perhaps even a Gypsy's eyes, he twisted one of the shells and stood back as the case swung forward.

The startled "O" formed on Lightning's lips was worth the risk he took, or so Traveler judged. "Come inside," he beckoned. "See if this catches your fancy, pretty lad," he added it without intention, but found himself pleased at the wide-eyed look Lightning gave him.

The boy stepped inside Traveler's hidden room, and stopped stock-still, blocking the entrance.

"There. How does this strike you?" Traveler prompted.

"I... I..." Lightning seemed lost for words, and well he might be.

Traveler's hideaway was a cave of wonders. Enchanted, of course, and a thick curtain drawn across his long-abandoned magical working room, but no less a marvelous sight for all that.

Lightning shook his head, mute. He swallowed the wealth of beauty in with hungry eyes. No windows, but a vast array of battered copper lamps. Scattered on a dozen small stands, they served to shed brightly-defining or softly-flattering shadows. Despite the warm weather, the stone walls kept this room a bit on the cool side for comfort, and a small fire crackled in a stone hearth, safe behind an ancient ironwork grate.

Vast piles of cushions, pillows, and soft mounds of fabric in rich, jewel-colored shades covered almost every available surface. They cried out to be touched, stroked, rested upon. Aye, and Traveler had even draped lengths of crushed velvet over the pale cream-painted walls to further entice the eye.

He tucked his thumbs in his belt and leaned against the doorframe, grinning at Lightning. "Well, now. What do you think?"

"I've never seen anything to compare," he whispered, finding words at last. "How did you do this?"

Traveler shrugged nonchalantly. "I like beautiful things as well as any other Gypsy."

"Do you, then?"

"Oh, aye." Traveler let himself do as he itched to, resting his hand on Lightning's lean shoulder, appreciating the warmth of his skin. "I like you."

Lightning turned about to face him, soot-ringed eyes wide. "Do -- do you?"

"Very much. I speak only the truth, as a Gypsy should." Strangely driven, Traveler placed two of his fingers beneath Lightning's chin and tipped it up. "Here, I'll be showing you how much."

"Oh." Lightning's pupils dilated. "*Oh.*"

"No fear," Traveler soothed. "I'll not hurt you, on my word."

Lightning licked his lips, and Traveler could not help but chase the youth's pink tongue. He bent his head and pressed their mouths together, meaning only the most chaste of kisses, but found himself crushing Lightning to him, plundering that enticing cavern with his tongue.

Lightning moaned into Traveler's mouth. He sagged a bit, then shored himself up by grasping Traveler's arms. And as he didn't protest the roughness of Traveler's kiss, Traveler grew bolder and began to thrust his tongue in and out of Lightning's mouth, a mimicry of what his cock ached to do with Lightning's arse.

All too soon, and disappointingly, Lightning pulled away to stare at Traveler. "Do you feel it?" he questioned, as if a great deal hung on Traveler's response. "The enchantment?"

"Only the charm in your lips and tongue," Traveler answered honestly, hoping for another chance to kiss that tempting mouth.

Lightning drew back, going shuttered again. "I should not have come," he said, voice flat. "There's a mistake here. I'll bother you no longer, Traveler. I remember the path out, and I'll be on my way."

Traveler's own temper flared. The hells Lightning would, coming in Traveler's home dressed to seduce and kissing him with abandon only like to what he'd felt when he crept in and Lightning let down his walls.

"Nay," he growled, seizing Lightning by the waist and holding him fast. "You're not leaving me here now, pretty one."

And he kissed the youth again to make sure Lightning knew he meant what he said.

No one would be going anywhere, oh no, not until this mystery was settled between them.

Chapter Six

Ah, but Lightning turned soft as a light spring rain when a man wrested the upper hand out of his proud grasp. Beneath the force of Traveler's kiss, his muscles, bow-string taut, melted like sweet beeswax candles. He moaned -- in despair or pleasure, Traveler couldn't tell -- and clung to Traveler, slender fingers digging in almost too hard.

Traveler didn't mind a bit of pain so long as he'd got his point across. As he growled and took Lightning by the back of his head, deepening their kiss, he suspected he might finally be making himself clear.

There was much and much he didn't understand about Lightning, aye. One thing remained for certain sure: he'd a desperate craving for the Gypsy youth.

Might even be, given the way Lightning went so pliant in Traveler's arms, he would have a chance to ease some of his hunger.

With an effort, Traveler reined in his passion enough to clear his lust-addled mind a touch. He'd not chance any blame or derision now, nay. If they did this, he needed to know Lightning wanted him for sure and certain. So he'd deal plainly as any Gypsy should, despite the temptation to just throw the lad down on the nearest cushion and have his way.

Traveler pulled out of their kiss, grinning as Lightning whimpered at their parting. "Look at me," he ordered. He didn't use any of his magics to get Lightning's attention, but aye, he didn't need them. Lightning stared at him through hazy eyes, lips parted ever so enticingly.

"What?" Lightning asked, the effort to summon speech clearly difficult. "Why did you stop?"

Traveler ran his thumb down the delicate line of Lightning's jaw. "Because I'll not press this suit if it'll please you ill in the long run."

"Why would I... oh." Lightning blinked. He grew half-wary again. "I'd near to forgotten myself," he mused, probably to himself but still scrambled enough not to realize Traveler would be hearing his words. "Mayhap this splits the hairs too fine, but oh..."

Traveler kept up his light touch. "I can hear you," he said gently. Lightning gave him a startled look. "You were thinking out loud, lad. And you spoke of things that give me pause. Are you under taboo or some sort of vow?"

Lords of the Road, did I push Lightning, all-unknowing, too far the night before?

Traveler didn't think so. Lightning had stopped him before they went all the way down Pleasure's Path. "Come, now," he encouraged. "Tell me where I stand, and if it's a secret it bides safe with me. I give you my word."

Lightning looked torn between flinging himself at Traveler and jumping far out of his reach. "Not taboo," he allowed after a pause. "But a vow, aye. I am sworn to remain a virgin until I find my -- well, until I've found the one I'm meant for."

"But how do you define virginity?" Traveler pressed. "Do you deny yourself the touch of others altogether, or have we a bit of room to play?" He chuckled. "I think you know what sort of games I have in mind."

The lad went dusky in his cheeks. He looked deliberately away from Traveler's face -- still, for sure and certain he took a longing peek down at the swollen cock tenting Traveler's trews as he turned away. Traveler counted this longing glance a good sign.

But if Lightning were under a strict vow, he'd be faced with making an apology for what he'd already done, and made to deny himself the pleasures his body ached for in this moment. "Tell me," he requested, neither threatening nor betraying his desperate need in his mild tones. "Trust me."

Lightning let out a soft breath. He wasn't accustomed to speaking of such things, Traveler felt sure, and he admired the lad's guts if he were going to answer the question.

"It's a long story," he said at last. "My family, small as it was, recognized as how a man would have needs. Still, I've held to the letter of the law laid down in my vow. No man has touched me except --" He broke off with a deeper blush.

So he didn't want to admit to what he'd

tasted the afternoon before. Pride, perhaps, or shame? Belike he didn't want Traveler to think him a wanton? "But a man who desired so might touch you in some ways, if not others?" Traveler pushed. "Explain, I beg."

Lightning cocked an eyebrow at the word "beg". Oh-ho, he wasn't immune to the charms of holding his own power over a man's head, was he? Traveler would have to teach him a lesson or two about such, were it allowable.

"There may be...touching," he allowed, hands straying toward Traveler even as he spoke. "Mouths. Fingers. Kisses. Touches. But no man may penetrate me unless -- until --"

Traveler laid a finger over Lightning's lips. "I've heard enough. And unless you stop me, pretty one, I'll be doing everything I can think of without crossing the line. Say me aye or say me nay, but do it now."

Lightning hesitated, torn. This wasn't playing fair, but Traveler slyly slipped beneath Lightning's fitted red velvet shirt and laid his hand over the lad's leather-encased cock, hard as stone in his palm and more than willing to play. Traveler rubbed the heel of his hand up and down Lightning's swollen length and leaned close enough to flicker his tongue in one of Lightning's ears. "Aye or nay," he breathed. "I'll show you delights you never even dreamed of."

The lad arched into Traveler's touch, hissing a breath between his teeth. "Oh, Lords -- good -- so good --"

"It can be better," Traveler promised.

"And that is what frightens me." Lightning

caught Traveler with his luminous gaze. "If we...if I... I'm not knowing what to do."

"Then let me be your teacher. Are you saying 'aye', pretty one?" Traveler pressed his lips to Lightning's temple. "Let me hear you speak the word."

"So help me and forgive me. Aye. Aye, do as you will." Lightning grasped Traveler's arms, leaning against the bulk of his chest. "I am yours, to a point, and for now."

"Good enough for me," Traveler agreed, and fell to teaching Lightning everything he knew about all pleasures of the flesh save one.

Ah, but he'd enjoy this, he would.

They began with Traveler doing naught but holding Lightning, breathing in his scent. He smelled of the salty sea, and underneath that a herbal soap of the sort a Gypsy might keep to trade. *So, he brought out the fine stuff to cleanse himself with? I wonder...did he come here hoping this might happen?*

Lightning squirmed as Traveler ran his nose down the youth's neck. "Tickles," he complained. "Prickles. You've not shaved."

"I'd thought to be alone today. Now hush." Traveler began to use his lips for something other than forming words, kissing a trail down Lightning's throat. The soft skin felt like silk, and when he sucked hard blood rose to the surface ever so beautifully. Lightning might take a bit of teasing for bearing the welts, but it pleased Traveler to put his mark on the youth. He rubbed that tender flesh with his stubbly cheek for good measure, a touch of beard-burn as a subtle clue that the pleasure

Faire Grounds

Lightning took was with a proper man.

He lifted up a bit to admire his work. Mmm, such a pretty look on the lad. And if the slight quickening of Lightning's breath was anything to go by, he'd enjoyed Traveler's mouth on him much as Traveler had liked the tasting.

Now, what next? Skin. Yes, I want skin. Traveler tugged at Lightning's fine scarlet tunic. The youth blinked in confusion. Such an innocent, and wouldn't it be fun teaching him a thing or three? "I'd have you take this off, this and your trews," Traveler whispered, teasing Lightning with a husky hint of things to come that he'd surely like better still. "They're fitted so tight, though, and I'd not rip or tear if I could avoid such."

Humor glinted in Lightning's quick smile. "They can't be damaged."

Can't they, now? Traveler felt the misty touch of the youth's own peculiar enchantments brush over him, but shrugged them off. He'd think on magics another time.

"You'd like to be bared before me," Traveler murmured, sliding the tunic up Lightning's chest. "You want me to see what's hidden beneath your finery."

He saw uncertainty written on Lightning's features. "I've never..."

"No fear nor shame," Traveler chided. He pressed his aching groin against Lightning's and rocked their hips together for the pleasure of hearing Lightning gasp. "I'm certain sure I'll like what I see."

Lightning shuddered. "Do as you will," he said in a whisper. "No fear. No shame."

"None at all," Traveler soothed. And no chances at a second thought or two, either. He guided Lightning through raising his arms to strip the tunic off, and while he might have liked a moment or two to admire the hard, lean muscles in Lightning's chest, he gave them only a lingering glance while he made for the fancy lacings of his trews.

When he laid hands on Lightning's groin, the lad began to moan as if he couldn't help himself, rocking into Traveler's touch. Traveler chuckled. So responsive. So passionate. If this was what lay beneath Lightning's prickles, then his persistence in getting past them was well worth all his efforts.

"Easy, now, easy," Traveler soothed as he undid the cords around Lightning's waist, those which held his trews closed. "Take a deep breath and count ten while I do this, now, so you don't spend too early." Youth did have its way of making a man quick off the mark.

He waited until Lightning began to obey, then slid the leather trews off his lad's hips and eased them down his legs, very fine with lean muscle, and all but hairless. So smooth, so fine.

Traveler did love a man not only pretty in face, but in body.

He knelt at Lightning's feet and tapped his ankles. The boy bit his lip and mumbled something, more than like an apology for not thinking, as he lifted one foot and then the other so Traveler could ease the trews completely off.

Once bare, he began to quiver, his hands

curling into fists. "Shh, shh," Traveler crooned. "No fear, no shame. You're beautiful, and if I'm the first to tell you this, then I count myself a lucky man. So lovely you are that I can't resist a taste." He grasped Lightning by the calves and began to kiss, lick, and suck his way up one thigh.

"Undo your hair," Traveler suggested impulsively. "I've a craving to see it loose about you, like a veil."

"You what?"

Traveler kissed one knee. "Humor me. Let down your hair."

He waited, tickling a sensitive spot behind one knee as Lightning lifted his braid and began to undo the weave. He seemed confused, aye, but as that glorious silky mane came loose he gave a sigh of pure sensual pleasure and tossed his head.

Oh, marvelous, marvelous. Better than Traveler had hoped. "Pretty lad," he approved, resuming his path up Lightning's leg. The brush of the loosened, soft black hair swept against his cheeks, inflaming his desire.

Lightning trembled hard as Traveler drew nigh to his cock -- and it was just as fine and upstanding an organ as he'd seen the day before, well worth admiring a second time. Traveler nuzzled in beneath Lightning's wrinkled sac and gave the pouch a quick lick just to tease.

Lightning groaned.

His limited experience would have him expecting Traveler's mouth on his prick next. Traveler wouldn't have minded one bit, but he feared Lightning would find his mouth familiar and then the game would be up.

Lords of the Road, what *had* possessed him the day before?

Ah, but he knew of something just as good, possibly even better, if Lightning didn't bolt away from the shock. He'd ease the youth into his plan, then, gentle him down. "Lie yourself across the pillows behind you," Traveler ordered. "They're soft enough to be a treat, and firm enough to prop you up for what I want."

"And when I am on my back, what will you do with me?" Lightning asked with a faint tremble.

"Something better than your best dream. Lie down, now. Yes, just so," Traveler approved as Lightning lowered himself onto a stack of green velvet cushions. There weren't quite enough for him to stretch full-length, leaving his legs dangling from the knee.

Perfect.

"Do you trust me?" Traveler queried as he rubbed Lightning's calves to soothe his no-doubt quaking nerves. Virgins were a treat, to be sure, but one had to take great care with them. "Do you believe I'll not cause you any harm?"

He heard Lightning swallow and saw him nod.

"Lift your legs, then. Spread them wide for me. No shame. Prop your feet upon the pillows to brace them, and let me look my fill. No shame."

Lightning's breathing quickened and he did

as he'd been told with wanton eagerness. Thus opened for him, Traveler could all the better smell Lightning's rich musk twined with the scent of soap. The soap, he ignored, all the better to focus on the smell of pure man.

Pressing his nose against Lightning's pendulous sac, he inhaled deeply.

"Traveler!" Lightning sounded scandalized -- but eager, aye, and not as if he minded this a whit.

"You smell divine. Should I not appreciate the fragrance?"

"Nay... I mean, aye... I mean, I never knew men would like this smell."

"And why not? 'Tis the scent of arousal, and to know that the man you want is anxious for your touch...ah, now there's a heady brew." Traveler grasped Lightning's cock -- he could do that much at least -- and swiped off the pearling drops of moisture gathering at his slit. He sucked them into his mouth and made an appreciative noise. "You taste as good as you smell."

"Traveler," Lightning breathed.

"Aye, 'tis me." Traveler adjusted the cushions just *so,* moving Lightning's legs an inch or so this way and that, punctuating his adjustments with kisses on his balls. He knelt back and declared himself satisfied.

Thus spread, Lightning's arse cheeks were parted and his tightly puckered hole exposed to Traveler's avid gaze. To tease, Traveler blew a stream of warm air over the virgin entrance.

Lightning moaned, then flinched.

"Traveler, you're not -- my vow."

"And this won't be breaking a word you've given," Traveler reassured. "It's not my cock I plan to put in there, pretty one."

He waited for Lightning to process the notion. "Oh!" he whispered in shock. "Do men actually...and they like it?"

"They love it, or at least I do. Let me taste you."

"Could I stop you? Could I stop me? No." Lightning arched, offering up his pucker. "Do it."

Traveler wasted no time. He wanted to drive Lightning mad, so he did, and he'd never met a man who didn't enjoy this to his maximum endurance. One hand on either of Lightning's soft inner thighs to keep them apart, he dove forward and traced his tongue around the tightly wrinkled hole.

Lightning howled.

Oh, oh, he was sensitive. Traveler would wager that were he given the chance, as how Lightning could be one of those rare men who'd climax from penetration alone. Truth, it was his cock aching to be in there instead of his tongue, but this was a fine game.

He licked again, and chortled as Lightning keened.

Lightning never once ceased his noise as Traveler plundered his sweet arse as thoroughly as he was allowed. After teasing him for a good while with sweeps of his tongue, savoring the strong flavor, getting his lad's pucker good and wet, he paused just long enough to make Lightning wail with frustration, and thrust his tongue inside.

Lightning's wail changed to a scream. He bucked and arched, muscles tightening till they shook, but Traveler showed him no quarter. He stabbed his tongue in and out of Lightning's hole and held on tight until Lightning choked out words which made no sense and came in thick spurts, some landing in Traveler's hair.

Traveler held the youth steady until he'd emptied himself of seed, then drew back and laughed kindly. "I take it you enjoyed this, eh?"

A snarl was his reward. Ah, but he'd learned to interpret the nuances of Lightning's noises, and took no offense.

But it was time Lightning learned another thing or two himself. The boy lay limp as a dolly, clearly not thinking of his partner's pleasure. Selfish, selfish, with ignorance his only excuse.

Traveler determined to teach him better.

"Come," he ordered, standing and seizing Lightning's hands. "On your feet." He glanced about. "Go and lean against the wall."

"My legs won't carry me yet," Lightning protested, though he let himself be drawn upright.

Traveler gave his taut arse a spank, just as he'd longed to do. "They'll hold you good and proper. Up against the wall, and make haste."

Lightning stumbled a bit, but did make his way to where he'd been directed and braced himself there, arse thrust out unconsciously in perfect position. "What happens now?"

"You've a need to learn about give and take,

you do. Never leave a lover wanting, lad. But since you didn't know, I'd wager, I'll lead the dance again."

Lightning bobbed his head in drunken agreement, still giddy from his climax. "As you say," he agreed, and wasn't it a sweet triumph to hear him so meek? For true, Traveler felt the need to purr as Luck did after hunting and catching some fine bit of prey.

Traveler jerked at the lacings of his own trews, careless in his haste, and eased his plain trousers down his hips, where they fell to the knee. Good enough. His cock sprang out, leaking in its eagerness to have some play. Welladay, what he had in mind should satisfy.

They'd need no oil for this. The slickness of his cock and the saliva left over from his tasting the boy's hole would make things easy. "Stand still, now," Traveler whispered. "I'm not coming inside, but I am going to enjoy your arse."

"What?" Lightning twisted around for a confused look. "How?"

Sweet mercy, how his naiveté never ceased to amuse. "Like so. And here, for the sake of my own pleasure, something in addition." Grasping the heavy weight of Lightning's hair, Traveler cast it over his own shoulder as one would a silken shawl.

Lightning drew in a sharp breath. "You..."
"Aye. Me."
"You bind us together with my hair."
"I do, and with this." Traveler slid his aching dick between the crease of Lightning's arse and began to move against him without

any further warning, thrusting into the slippery seam in search of the friction he craved.

Lightning laughed, a rippling sound Traveler suspected he could grow to love. Quick to catch on, he was, tightening the muscles of his arse so Traveler had to work at it, but enjoyed himself all the more for needing a good hard effort. There was friction, if you liked!

His own climax built up thick and heavy in his balls. Truth, he'd have liked this to take all day, but Lightning had tormented him much too far and the youth was a devilishly clever natural at this part of the game.

Traveler sank his teeth into Lightning's shoulder, swore fit to turn the air blue, and climaxed in a messy, splattering blaze of triumph. Lightning cried out as he felt Traveler's seed pulse against his entrance, then moaned and rolled his hips.

Traveler took a moment to catch his breath, then slipped out of Lightning's crease and leaned against him, wrapping his arms around that lean chest. "Now," he said, voice rich with amusement, "have you enjoyed yourself? And have we broken any rules you know of?"

Lightning raised his head wobblingly, near-drunk, and gave a happy-sounding sigh. "My vow holds good, though you divided that particular hair *very* finely." He laughed again. "I could almost feel that...feel that..."

The youth grew still. Not stiff, but not loose and easy as a man should be after taking such pleasure. Traveler had no idea what might be going on in his mind, but bedamned if he'd let this end quite yet.

"Back to the pillows," he coaxed, tugging Lightning along. "They're comfortable enough for a rest, and if you're like any man I've ever known, you'll want a nap more than anything now."

Lightning gave Traveler a searching look as he drew his hair back to his own shoulders. Peculiarly, intently searching...and confused. "A taste of slumber," he agreed after a pause. "You're right, it would be good."

"Then come with me." Traveler was stubbornly determined not to let Lightning bolt this soon. "On the pillows, yes." He guided Lightning down. "Rest you, and have no fear. I'll wake you in plenty of time to sail back by good light."

"Aye," Lightning mumbled as he nestled among the pillows. He hesitated, then said, quickly, "Thank you."

Traveler managed a weary chuckle. Truth, he felt more than a bit worn out himself. "Believe me, no thanks are needed; I had a goodly fill of my own pleasure." He allowed himself a lingering caress of Lightning's soft, loose hair. "Sleep," he encouraged -- but Lightning was already gone.

Pretty lad, Traveler thought as he stroked Lightning with a freer hand, lightened by the easing of his cares. *Sleep you well, fair Lightning. I think you'll dream sweet dreams of me, aye? As I'll dance with you in my own sleep visions.*

He could not have been further wrong.

Chapter Seven

No sooner had Lightning's eyes closed in sleep than he found himself plunged into a dream -- no, yet another vision. Ordinary dreams lacked the sharp edges of clarity, the smells of his caravan, and the feel of smooth wood beneath his recently pleasured behind.

"Greetings to you, Lightning, my son," a voice Lightning knew all too well spoke gently. "It's been long and long a time since last we met. But you know me still, don't you?"

Lightning gaped as he stared at Slipstream, good old beloved Father Slipstream, taking his ease on the caravan's big pallet decorated with the thick quilt he and Horsetail had favored.

"You look..." he said in wonder. "You're young again." His fingers itched to touch the skin unmarred by wrinkles, the full cheeks no longer withered with sickness and age. "How can this be?"

Slipstream chuckled. "In the lands to which I have passed, there is no one old or feeble. Horsetail sends his greetings, by the bye."

A shiver ran down Lightning's spine. This was a vision for sure and true, but this tested the limits of with what he could cope.

Faire Grounds

Slipstream had died long since, he and Horsetail both. Visits from the dead were to be respected, as they only came back when those they cared about needed guidance, but Lightning felt a growing sense of dread. What if Slipstream had come to punish him for the frolics he'd indulged in with Traveler, when he wasn't -- quite -- sure of the man as yet?

Slipstream lifted a hand. "Easy, son. There's no need for the fear writ upon your face. I've not come as an avenging spirit, but only as a humble visitor to lend an ear and, as I sensed you needed, a bit of comfort." He grinned. "In truth, do I look as if I mean you harm?"

The uneasiness did not go away complete, but Lightning felt his terror fade a bit. He breathed easier, and even laughed a bit. Slipstream had been a dear old soul, but in death he was homely as ever he'd been. There couldn't have been a taller, skinnier, plainer man in all the kingdoms or villages they'd traveled through.

Slipstream knew he wasn't handsome, but didn't care a whit. Settled on his pallet, he looked like a long-legged spider with a horse's face, and Lightning had never known anyone to match his kind nature, not even Horsetail, who'd been given to being gruff.

"People trust an ugly Gypsy more," he'd told Lightning once upon a time. "They figure their women are safe from me, which I should well know, and they're more likely to be free in their approach. All the better profit for us, eh?"

But that had been then, and this was now.

"Tell me, then, dear son. What troubles you?" Slipstream settled himself more comfortably, and grunted in satisfaction, a sound Lightning had rarely heard during his father's mortal life when he had more often than not been in pain. Horsetail and Slipstream had been of a fair age when they'd taken him in. "I am here to listen."

Lightning started to speak, but the words he would have voiced tumbled one over the other in his mind and tied his tongue in a hard knot. He spread his hands helplessly.

"Ah, I know that look of old. You've no idea how to begin." Slipstream nodded sagely. "I'll start off with what I know, shall I? I can see such things now, and your aura -- the life-force that surrounds you -- is all a-flare from your troubled mind and many a doubt." He narrowed his eyes. "Younger and Peddler's enchantment holds yet, and I spy that it has caught you in its snare. Have you met your soul-mate, then?"

"I -- perhaps -- I'm not sure," Lightning managed to spill out. "He's not what I expected, Father. He seems to feel none of the same connection, not like the stories have foretold, and worse, he's a Gypsy gone to ground, a deserter of the road. How can such a man be my soul-mate?"

"Hmm. That is a thorny problem, and no mistake." Slipstream hummed as he thought, then tilted his head to a side. "May I touch you, Lightning? There'll be neither pain nor harm, but with my hand on your head I might read you better."

Faire Grounds

Lightning didn't care for the idea, but his trust in Slipstream grew by the moment. How could he fear the spirit of his father when he'd been so gentle? "Do what you will and what pleases you."

"My thanks." Slipstream placed nimble fingers on both of Lightning's temples. He hummed again, tune changing from time to time. Lightning waited patiently to see what the old -- no, young -- man would say.

Self-restraint only went so far, at least in Lightning's case. He forbore so long as he could, but found himself blurting: "Well? What do you see?"

Slipstream clicked his tongue. "Impatient as ever, aren't you?" He removed his hands and folded them in his lap. "This man -- Traveler, eh? An odd name for a man to keep when he's put down roots -- he *is* your soul-mate, my son. I know not why Younger and Peddler's enchantments have chosen him for you, but there it lies. You belong at his side, and he at yours."

"But how is that possible, when I belong to the road and he has forsaken journeys?" Lightning asked in despair. "We can never find a life together so long as neither of us change our ways."

"Lightning," Slipstream chided. "I've told you I know nothing more, and you should not doubt my word. This is something, I ken, you will have to work out for yourself. But a bit of advice, if you'll permit? Tell this Traveler the truth, and soon. It would be well if you were truly joined before your twenty-and-first birthday. I can read a bit of him, besides, and he has his own doubts about you despite what you've shared together." Slipstream twinkled mischievously. "That hungry for him, were you, that you'd risk so much?"

Lightning blushed and looked down.

Slipstream chortled. "Nay, nay, the man is your soul-mate, so there's no harm done. I'll bid you farewell for now, but remember what I've said. Tell him, Lightning. Tell him soon."

He began to fade. Lightning reached out, as fearful of Slipstream's departure as he had been at the man's appearance. "No, Father, no! Don't go."

"I must." Slipstream had turned half to mist, and his voice sounded far away. "Know that we love you, Horsetail and I. We will always watch over you, beloved son..."

And Slipstream was gone, leaving Lightning trapped in the caravan. The vision turned to a nightmare, air pressing in so tight and stuffy Lightning found it hard to breathe. He stood and whirled about, looking for an exit, but the caravan was sealed tight with wood roundabout. A coffin.

In his dreams, Lightning began to scream...

* * *

Lying snug beside Lightning, Traveler found himself dreaming as well. Not visions, thought they might as well have been, aye, for how real they seemed to him.

He was a Prince again, Heir to his father's kingdom, and sitting at an elegantly carved stone table, sunk deep in thought. Thoughts that pleased him ill. The date of his arranged marriage was drawing nigh, and with each day that passed his unhappiness increased.

Being wed and bound to a woman -- well, such was hardly in his true nature, not that he'd ever breathed a word contrariwise to anyone trusted or mistrusted. He'd shame his father and sully his name in the gossip sure to spring up like springtime weeds. He dared not be his true self, and as a result had found himself tied to the Lady Rosalind.

In truth, he'd even pushed himself to get under her skirts to prove his desire for her, though his pleasure in the act had been less than nil. She'd seemed happy enough despite his poor performance, and kissed him as reward. Rumors flew after their dalliance, but those would cause no harm.

After all, a young man should be lusty when faced with a fair Lady like his betrothed.

Bored, Traveler -- or Janos, as he'd been -- plucked a mirror from the top of his stone table and murmured the words of a scrying spell. He'd a mind to see Rosalind again, to try and convince himself once more again that wedding her would not be such a bad thing. He'd hardly perfected his skills at magic, not having let anyone know of those inclinations either, but he could manage a simple mirror trick.

Rosalind's image appeared in the glass. So far as he could tell, she sat at a table of her own, primping and preening with her carefully arranged curls and narrowly examining the effects of the paints she wore.

"You've a nerve," another woman whispered in admiration. "Such a bold plan, Rosalind!"

Janos' affianced scoffed as she began to remove her ornate jewelry. "Lovely, but too heavy for comfort," she commented. "And yes, it is a brave strike, but I know what I know about Janos. He's kept the secret well-hidden, but in truth, he prefers men to women. Clear enough after his pitiful attempt at making love." She snickered. "The wretch could barely raise his organ when he approached me!"

"It's not well thought of, nor proper for princes, but truly there's no harm in men loving other men, or so say the Laws."

"Yes, but as Heir and my betrothed, do you think he wants such a secret revealed? A word here and there and his reputation will be ruined."

"But do you want such a thing? I'd think your desire would be for just the opposite."

"Exactly so. But the man looks sour as a lemon and grows tart as unripe persimmon as our nuptials approach. He may be driven to find a way to break our agreement and live as a bachelor again, free to pursue his tastes. And I'll not have that, not when I'm set to be Queen after Janos' father dies."

"And thus your plan?"

"Quite. He's ignorant enough of women that he'll believe me when I tell him our coupling got me with child. He'll marry me quick enough then, likely with the point of the King's sword at his back -- and my own

Faire Grounds

father's, I'm sure."

"But what will he do when your belly doesn't swell with a babe?"

"I don't foresee any problems," Rosalind said carelessly. "When I first bleed after we're bound together, I'll take to my bed in artful great pain, and summon a midwife. They're a foolish lot around these parts, little better than horse-curers. Who'll be able to tell the difference between losing a child and an ordinary cycle? Janos is likely to be dismayed, but we'll be tied together and he'll have no choice to bide within our marriage."

"Cunning as well as bold," Rosalind's confidante breathed in admiration.

"I'm nobody's fool, and I won't be toyed with. This marriage is my means to a life of luxury and the eventual title of Queen." The cold *clink* of Janos' affianced's jewelry as it dropped piece by piece into her safe-keeping chest sounded to him like taps on the lid of a coffin. "I'll never want for anything as Janos' wife, except perhaps a good time in bed. I need not want for that either, really. If I'm discreet, I can take a lover who'll please me. Yes, my friend. I have Janos exactly where I want him. Poor fool, but it's his own fault in the end. I will not be stopped."

Janos slammed the mirror onto its front, with Rosalind's cruel smile taunting him. His head whirled, but just as his "Lady" had declared her lack of unwillingness to be played, he found himself grinding his teeth in determination to avoid the same fate.

And although it spelled the beginning of the

end for him, Janos sent Rosalind a note before an hour had passed.

His letter was short and to the point:
Traitoress,

I know the truth and how you planned to fool me. If you do not leave this keep before sunset, I will see to it that everyone else knows as well how faithless you are.

I mean what I say, betrayer. Do not test me.

No longer yours,

Janos

* * *

Janos grunted in his sleep, desperate to flee the nightmarish memory. He turned over on his side, pushing pillows willy-nilly, but to no avail. A second dream fell upon him with sharp claws, as if it had been lying impatiently in wait for its chance to attack.

* * *

"No!" Janos' younger brother Andrei howled, face going purple with rage. "You sit here and tell me this pervert remains the heir? The scandal alone will ruin us." He glowered with deadly determination. "Janos deserves to be spitted on the nearest spike, but I'll be damned if I don't see what my own blades can do."

"You could try," Janos replied coldly. He was easily twice the swordsman than Andrei was, and he had the advantage of a cool head.

Both brothers ignored the frantic chattering

Faire Grounds

of their advisors, who'd hoped for a far more placid conference. Their father, the King, sat silent but darksome as a storm cloud at the head of the table. No telling which way his mind bent.

"I'll bow my head to no man with such unnatural desires," Andrei hissed. "The King that would be shall be a laughingstock. And who's to be his heir if he produces none of his own? A cousin? Father, think of the infighting. If Janos has not already destroyed us by then, the battle among our kin surely will."

"And I suppose a whoring, drinking, spendthrift beast like you is better suited to rule?" Janos pushed his chair back with a loud scrape and stood, facing his father the King. "I'm done with this. Take Andrei as your Heir, if it pleases you, and I'll be on my way."

The King regarded his firstborn son with cool eyes that, Janos noticed for the first time, contained traces of distaste. "Go."

And Janos had left the selfsame night, Andrei's threat ringing in his ears: "I'll kill you yet if ever I get the chance, offal!"

He'd never gone back, not even in his journeys on the road, swinging wide about and far out of his way to avoid his father's lands. Gossip still reached him, though, and he learned that as he'd foretold, when Andrei took over the crown he speedily began a steady ruination of a once-steady throne.

Damned if he'd let himself care, though. He'd traveled and learned enough magic from the Gypsies to be called a proper wizard, and come to a stop at the edge of the world to live out his days in peace behind a shield forged of sorcery. Not for fear, no.

He simply wanted to be left alone.

And alone he had been, until there came Lightning...

* * *

Traveler sprang up with a hoarse cry. "Lightning!"

He turned to the youth and saw his eyes fly open, full of fear that he suspected was a mirror of his own. He scooted back hastily, putting a distance between them, and spoke before he thought. "Who are you? *What* are you? I can feel the enchantments clinging to you like spider webs; I have known they were there since we met. What do you want from me?"

Lightning made no protest and voiced no questions. He simply sat upright and composed himself with such dignity that he might be dressed in his finery again, and met Traveler's gaze with only the slightest tremor of nerves and more than a taste of his familiar prickliness.

"I am descended from Gypsies bound by ancient enchantments," he said, calm as still water. "The spell seeks out our soul-mates and binds us one to the other. This must happen before our twenty-and-first birthday, or the power that protects us will be shattered." His gaze held steady. "The enchantment has chosen you, Traveler, as my mate."

At first Traveler found himself too shocked to move, to speak, aye, almost to breathe. Images from his first nightmare filled his mind, Rosalind's betrayal and the dread he'd felt at being locked and chained. "You lie," he accused.

"I do not. My word as a Gypsy that I tell only the truth, believe me or believe me not." Lightning's proud chin lifted in defiance.

His word. From what Traveler knew of Lightning, aye, from what he'd been denied due to Lightning's vows, he took everything he spoke serious as the grave.

Bound. Tied by enchantment. *So, now I know what's kept bringing us together. Why I let him in. Why I've felt such a hunger for his body... and a craving for his approval? Nay -- his love.*

"There is no breaking this?" Traveler asked hoarsely.

"None." Lightning crackled with indignation. "Am I that loathsome to you? Or had you pegged me as a quick tumble and nothing more?"

"I --" Traveler hesitated.

Lightning dealt him a blank, level stare. "I see." He stood, reaching for his cast-off tunic and trews. "So this is how the land lies."

"Nay, wait, wait." Traveler found himself reaching out to seize the lad. "It's my surprise talking, so it is."

"We are meant to be linked by love. Tell me and tell me true, Traveler, do you feel any such thing?" Lightning challenged. "Any hint at all?"

Love. Though the thought surprised him yet, Traveler could turn the notion over and over again in his head, and realize that if he did not yet love Lightning with his whole heart -- he *could*.

"What I feel...it could become love." And the thought frightened him half to death. He lived alone, he worked alone, he'd intended to grow old alone. More, he'd found his home on this island while Lightning seemed devil-bent for sticking to the road.

The problems seemed insurmountable. For all that, though, Traveler could not deny the bond between himself and this prickly young Gypsy. "Would a promise that I will try suit you?" he suggested. "Give me time. We both need space and days to come to grips with this, I think. There's more at stake than love, as I think you know."

Lightning gave a terse nod.

"Is my proposal acceptable?"

"It will do for now, but only a little while. We should be handfasted before my birthday, and that is less than a week away." Lightning found his clothing and began climbing into the garments gracefully as a cat while Traveler found his breath stolen once more.

"I see," was all he could say.

Lightning looked at him with the same cold blankness he'd once seen in his father's eyes. "Come to me when you've made your choice," he ordered. "But I'll not pine after you. If the enchantment breaks, it breaks, and I'll not mourn, but make my way as best I can."

Proud Lightning. Traveler's head swam with

Faire Grounds

thoughts darting quickly around as silverfish. Love? Not-love? Handfasting? Less than a week?

He forced a nod. This would require much thought, but -- "I'll come to you," he promised. "Whether to say yea or nay, I'll come."

"See you do." Dressed once again with no signs of their frenzied coupling save for his unbound hair, Lightning made for the door. He'd said he could find his own way out, and Traveler did not stop him.

At first.

Without his mind's permission, he blurted: "I will do what you ask of me."

Lightning stopped stock-still. Ever so slowly, he turned around to examine Traveler. "Will you, now?"

"With conditions. We still take our time to choose what way the wind will blow our future. No rushing into further decisions. And any secrets you glean, you keep to yourself. The knowledge of what my home is like, for one."

After consideration, Lightning nodded. "Acceptable. And when would you have us bound?"

Traveler could not think of any suitable date, so after a moment's struggle he shrugged. "When it pleases you best."

"Shall I find you on the faire grounds, then, or must needs I row out to your island again?"

More magic to be used, more chances of discovery, but he had to do what was called for. "On the night when your campfire burns solid blue, look for me in the morning." Lords of the Road, Traveler could scarce believe he was binding himself to such a bargain. Yet what was begun had best be done. "My vow do I give you on this."

"Good enough." Ah, but all of Lightning's softness had disappeared, and his prickles were out in full, pointed force. "We'll meet again on the day you choose."

He turned to leave. Prompted again by what he could not ken, Traveler blurted: "A kiss before you go? One kiss."

"I think not. You'll have kisses in plenty when we're wed; I've no doubt you'll see to that well enough, lusty as you are." Lords, Lightning made it sound like an insult when he'd been a wailing, writhing creature of lust himself so short a time before. He paused, then spit out two more words. "Thank you."

And with that, he turned and left. When his footsteps had faded and the front door of Traveler's home slammed shut, Traveler sank back amongst his pillows and stared at the ceiling in shock.

Luck, who'd likely sneaked in when Lightning took his leave, jumped up next to Traveler's head and said "Rrrowl." His catly voice came out laced with disgust.

"Not you, too." Traveler shoved Luck away with a shake of his head.

So. Bound once again.

Lightning, Lightning, what have you done to me? The price I've paid for a taste of paradise is far too dear, but you drew the promise from me. Pretty Lightning, how you've turned my life upside-down and that without

shame.
 No shame, hah!
 Traveler settled down with a long, rattling breath. "Welladay," he murmured to himself. "What tricks does Dame Fortuna have in store for me *next?*"

Chapter Eight

Three nights and three days had passed. Lightning waited stoically as he could. Had he confided in anyone, they might have been giving him dubious looks by now, doubting Traveler would make good on what he'd promised.

He gave me a Gypsy's word. Lightning crouched in front of his nightly campfire and prodded crossly at the crackling log, which, despite what he might wish, burned a yellow-orange snapping dance. His chin thrust out stubbornly. *Even if he's gone to Ground -- and I'll not think about that -- not yet -- he's still a Gypsy. He's bound by what he said, and he'll follow through.*

He will.

In the meantime, Lightning had waited and busied himself best as he might. Instead of waiting for folk to come and wheedle free samples of his teas, which Gypsies loved so well and got so rarely, he'd opened a large packet one night and taken the loan of Heartsease's kettle to brew enough for all to come and have a cup. Word had spread, and Grounders -- though they were watched carefully, aye -- came with grudging coins to

Faire Grounds

spend for the treat they almost never tasted either.

A few had threatened Lightning with accusations of thievery or witchcraft, claiming no Gypsy could lay his hands on so much leafy gold without a sticky hand or conjuring up dire spirits to fetch the tea for him.

He'd laughed those off, the other Gypsies backing him up until the Grounders went away with red cheeks, but afterwards they *had* looked at Lightning, and at his ancient-but-perfect caravan, and withdrawn a little from his company.

The rejection stung. *What will they do when they find out I mean to tie myself to a deserter?* Lightning hid his shudder. *I'll take everything as it comes, and fight each battle in its turn. I've done with dread and doubt. No more.*

He nodded firmly as he jabbed his makeshift poker, a solid branch trimmed down to a short pole, at the fire.

It blazed cheerfully at him, red and gold and utterly ordinary.

Lightning gave *whoof* of disgust and sat back on his hindquarters. Others could see him, had they a mind to be looking, so he kept his expression coolly blank to hide his thoughts. They troubled him, but he'd brook no curious questions it would not please him to answer.

For, although he'd done a merry business selling to Road-kin and to the occasional Grounder, Lightning had also spent as many hours as he could napping or asleep. He'd hoped Slipstream or even Horsetail would appear to him again, aching for the comfort of their presence and the wisdom of their counsel.

But, no, no, what did he do, without fail, when he laid himself down to sleep? He dreamed of Traveler, ever and always. Sometimes of their first meeting, when Lightning had felt the enchantment take hold, sometimes of how Traveler persisted on rescuing him from Grounders, but more often...

Aye, more often he found himself lost in dreams of himself spread out on Traveler's cushions, legs sprawled wide and a tongue where he'd never dreamed a man might want to put his face. He dreamed of the times they'd kissed and how it felt as if his bones were melting, or as if he'd been caught up in a hurricane of blasting passion.

He always sprang awake from these dreams with either sticky blankets or a solid wood he reached for without thinking. The feel of his own hand on his cock had always been enough to please him, but not now. He could not help but imagine Traveler's grip in place of his own, feeling once again the hot biting kisses that had left him bruised, and remembering how the man had stroked his hair.

When seed shot from his shaft, he shaped the same name with his lips, a desperate hoarse whisper: "Traveler!"

Much more of this, and Lightning felt he would burst with need.

He craved more. No -- he *needed* more. A mystery to him; he'd never been so desperate before. Then again, all he'd ever done was have a handsome lad catch his eye, trade a few quips, and later indulge in a light-hearted fantasy when he caught a few moments alone to stroke his own cock.

For sure and certain, what he and Traveler had done went beyond anything Lightning ever toyed with in fancy, much less in flesh. And he found that once he'd tasted of these pleasures, he burned for more.

Was sex an addiction? Did Traveler lace his touches with some magic of his own to make Lightning burn so for more time spent alone with the man?

Or was it just Traveler who made him weak with lust?

Restless, Lightning poked at his fire a third time. *Make haste,* he thought irritably. *What keeps you bound to your island and not coming to my side?*

Traveler had accepted the power of the enchantments. He'd understood what they meant to Lightning and the line from which he'd sprung. He'd sworn to obey the call of Younger's old spells.

Lightning stubbornly refused to doubt his -- his? Yes, his -- Gypsy's word.

He sat, and he waited, and he watched.

* * *

Three nights and three days had passed, yet Traveler's sense of -- shock, he supposed he might call this -- refused to fade. He'd tried to keep up with his work on the island, everything from tugging weeds out of the garden to strengthening his magical wards, but he always found himself lapsing into daydreams about Lightning's lithe, strong body and the comeliness of his face.

Earlier in this afternoon, Traveler had given up, disgusted. He went to sit on his front lawn in search of comfort from the richness of nature so kindly growing on the rocky island as he had made humble request once upon a time. Long and long ago the day seemed now, aye, yet he'd only been living in his adopted home for how long... perhaps five years?

The soft loam and springy grass refused to provide Traveler the ease he'd hoped for. All the same, he'd sat there until the sun went down, watching Luck chase after insects and, once, a fat mouse. Traveler had no idea how rodents found their way out to his abode, but in truth Luck grew fatter still on them, and he'd long ago shrugged it off as a quirk of the magics.

Despite himself, he chuckled. Wouldn't it just be the way of sorcery, tricksome as spells tended to be, that he had overlooked a small portal from the town irresistible to mice? If there were such a thing, he could pin the blame on Luck, greedy thing, and he'd no doubt, nay, as to how Luck might have picked up a trick or two to add to his own feline alchemy.

And speaking of the creature...

As the night began in earnest, Luck prowled up to Traveler and nudged the top of his head against Traveler's knee. His way of saying hello, and letting Traveler know he happened to be in a mood for company.

"Good lad," Traveler murmured, scratching between Luck's ears. A fit of whimsy struck him. "I've no one who I dare contact for advice. Would it please you to lend an ear?"

Luck drew back and blinked at him through luminous eyes. He tilted his head thoughtfully, then gave a deep chirrup.

"I'll be owing you a favor," Traveler offered formally, on the off chance that Luck really was more than an ordinary cat, or he were letting someone in to be of assistance. You never knew with his breed. "The story I have to tell is a long one, but I'll be quick to the point as I may."

Luck lifted one forepaw to lick and then rub across his face.

"Lightning. You've seen him when he visited this place. What did you think of the lad?"

Luck sneezed.

"Aye, he does get up your nose, doesn't he, then? Up your nose and under your skin. In truth, Luck, I cannot seem to stop myself from thinking on him. Cats do not blush, so I have no fear in confessing that when I sleep, I dream of him, so sweet and lithe in my arms, all his prickly quills laid flat. I relive the passion that blazed between us. I recall how he felt as I had my way, all a-quiver but eager as myself. We didn't go so far as two men might, but I've never taken greater pleasure, no, not even from fucking about with Lightlaugh and Fairlaugh or their like."

Luck blinked again, as if he were intrigued and wished for Traveler to go on.

"Lascivious thing, to want to know such details," Traveler chided. "No matter how I try to direct my thoughts elsewhere, he appears wherever I go. I smell his scent in my nostrils, I taste his flavor on my tongue, and I can all but feel his smooth skin and silky hair when I touch *corn*, for the sake of the Road Lords." He dropped his head into his hands. "Oh, I have it bad, aye?"

Luck purred, sounding smug.

"And I suppose you'd know all about these things, eh?" Traveler asked, then chuckled. Most would call it madness to seek counsel from a cat, but, well, what did he care? He walked alone without getting knotted up in the affairs of other men.

Or he had before, going on years of freedom now.

Luck settled in a pose of patient waiting. Traveler went on: "The tale Lightning told me of enchantments...it's solid. I need no augury, nor divination. It makes the tie I felt form between us when first we met make sense. But why? Anyone on Earth or beyond our ken should know I'm the last man a free-roving true-born Gypsy should be bound to. Why was I chosen?"

Luck twitched his whiskers.

"I could have said no," Traveler insisted. "Whence came the compulsion to agree? More of these enchantments, to which I would object -- I do not care for being manipulated -- or have I truly grown fond of the lad?" He shook his head. "Protest and joy tangle in my mind, and I'm unable to pull them apart."

Luck snorted disdainfully.

Traveler took umbrage. "I've no fear, so don't be thinking me a coward. I'm just sure as I can be this will all end in tears, as the Grannies often cluck their tongues and say. There's no logic or wisdom in this. And why should I fall in love? I've put such things long behind me."

Luck hissed. He raised a paw and struck Traveler's knee, sharp claws shredding through his thin workaday trews and scoring deep gashes into the skin beneath. "Ho there, friend!" Traveler protested as thick drops of blood welled to the cuts, which stung like a mother-loving bitch. "What's the idea?"

The cat gave him a narrow look, which Traveler could interpret without any guidance. *Idiot.*

Apparently having had enough of listening to Traveler's foolishness, the massive cat raised himself and stretched one solid limb at a time, mouth wide in a sharp pink yawn. He shook his fur and loped off, soon invisible in the darkness.

Traveler let out a sigh. "Truth, I am being a fool. I suspect the nature of these enchantments, and I doubt my own heart, but I've given my word, and although I am not Gypsy born I will not betray their codes of honor. Let's begin to be done with this, then."

Ever since Lightning had rowed away from his island, Traveler had taken care to keep a small pouch of powder tied to the waist of his trews, along with a stick of chalk around his neck. He didn't need much for such a simple spell, no. The only other thing he required, well, Luck had obtained that for him. His own blood.

Traveler squinted in the moonlight as he drew a careful circle on the grass. His pouch-full of powder was dumped in the center, the salt-sized crystals sparkling corundum blue. He firmed his lips as he brushed his fingers across his wounded knee and came up dripping with blood.

He thrust his gory hand into the powder and turned the crystals over and over, coating them with his life-fluid. "Find your way to the fire of the one to whom I've given my word," he whispered. True wizards generally needed no cantrips or any such rubbish; the spirits whom attended their mage-workings were quite capable of obeying simple commands. "Turn his fire blue as a signal that I will join him on the morrow. Go, now."

The crystals warmed in a flash to near searing heat, then cooled just as quickly.

It would be done, then.

Traveler bowed his head in acknowledgment of the step he'd taken, then summoned a breeze to blow away the powder. When it was gone, he rubbed his chalk circle from the grass and stood, albeit with a curse. Lords of the Road, Luck had given him some deep cuts.

He'd see to his wounds, and he'd try to get some sleep.

And on the morrow, he would change his life for-ever and ever.

* * *

Faire Grounds

Lightning had almost drifted into sleep, lulled by the soft noises from his fire and the streaming warmth. He'd rested overmuch and should not have been weary, but of a certainty the past few days had been trying to his mind.

He blinked sleepy eyes, gazing at the fire in a mix of depression and disgust.

Haste, Traveler, if you care for me at all, he thought, cross.

And as if the man himself had heard Lightning's voice at last, the fire flickered and new flames of pure, corundum blue sprang up to drown out the yellow and red. He blinked and rubbed his eyes, then pinched himself to be certain he hadn't fallen into a dream, but no, his fire burned blue.

Part of him wanted to give a cheer; another part gave grim acknowledgement; a third part knew he would get no sleep for a while. He had business to take care of.

Dousing his fire with a nearby bucket of water, Lightning stood and brushed off his sleeves. Well. He'd best get on with it, then, hadn't he?

* * *

Traveler rowed across to Mossy Rock in the half-light of dawn. He'd slept poorly, racked with nerves over what he intended to do, and although it might not have been wise, gotten on his way so soon as it were safe to travel the waters.

Luck had sat on the stone wall as Traveler freed his own boat of its moorings. The beastie's green eyes had nigh burned a hole in Traveler's back, but his purring had been loud enough to hear all the way down to the shore.

An uncanny creature, Luck. Traveler put little stock in omens, unlike many of his magic-kin, preferring to shape his own fate instead of cowering and forecasting doom when a raven flew overhead or calling for celebration should a flower bloom out of season.

All the same, he couldn't help but feel Luck's rumbling contentment was a sign that he had set himself to do the right thing.

The knowledge was strangely...comforting.

Traveler rowed on, searching the banks of Mossy Rock for a good place to moor his craft. His usual spots were roped off, no doubt by Grounders who'd hoped to deny as many Gypsies as possible from paddling out for a catch of fresh fish they'd prefer on their own dinner tables.

As he looked, he saw a trim, lean figure dressed in royal purple stride down to the stony banks. The wind off the sea blew his loosened hair into a wild mane around his head, black as the midnight sky.

Lightning.

Keen, wasn't he? Ah, well, Traveler supposed he would be too, were he in the lad's place. In his *own* place, he had to swallow down a knot of nerves -- and kept on rowing, determined not to lose courage now.

He'd do this as a man should.

And...ha-ha...after they were bound, he'd be able to do whatever he pleased with Lightning, wouldn't he? He could have those trim ankles locked around his back while he had his fill of

Faire Grounds

kisses, or show Lightning how to ride a man's cock -- ah, he suspected they'd both enjoy that a great deal -- or bend the proud young Gypsy over anything he pleased to take what he wanted.

He'd assert his place as alpha in their partnership, and teach his young mate a few more lessons, not only on how to please a man. There'd be no breaking of his spirit, which would be a shame, but he'd tease and torment and fuck some respect into Lightning, so he would.

Suddenly grinning with anticipation, Traveler stirred himself to row faster.

* * *

Lightning watched as Traveler found a decent spot of shore for his boat and lashed it in place with sturdy rope. He said nothing, but folded his arms across his chest and its thin purple tunic. Another raid on Slipstream's chest had provided him just the garments he needed to hold his head up high and proud on his nuptial day.

Traveler appeared to be wearing solid workaday clothes, but Lightning decided not to protest. He'd no time for arguments that would reach no agreeable end, as after some thought he'd deduced Traveler was a man who did things his own way and in his own time.

Takes his time, too, aye, doesn't he? Lightning gritted his teeth. *Here he comes. Now's the moment of truth, then. Let us see what we'll see.*

Lightning's life-mate said nothing until he'd drawn close enough for Lightning to see every line on his face. More than he'd remembered, but mostly smile-lines, which was heartening.

"How old are you?" he asked abruptly.

Clearly not the greeting Traveler had expected. He raised an eyebrow in curiosity. "Thirty-and-seven. Why?"

"Curiosity." Lightning shrugged. *Not quite twice my age, but close. Horsetail and Slipstream were not so far apart in years, nor have I heard of any such all the way back to Younger and Peddler. Yet another odd step in this dance.* "There's no need for speeches. We know why we've come together. Let's be on our way." He turned and began to walk up toward the faire.

"Hold, hold!" Traveler grabbed his shoulder. "Where are we going? What am I to do?"

Road Lords, the man sounded nervous as a fox in a room full of hunting dogs. Lightning hid a grin as he replied, "I've been busy this last night. The Gypsies are ready for us. We're heading for the heart of our kin's encampment, and there we'll be joined." He glanced over his shoulder to gauge Traveler's reaction. "There'll not be a long wait. Are you ready?"

Traveler squared his shoulders. "I am."

"Then follow me." Lightning's heart beat triple-time in his chest. He'd known all his life this moment would come one day, but he hadn't realized the day would be so daunting.

Nor had he expected himself to be tormented with relentless, blazing fantasies

Faire Grounds

about what would happen after he and his intended were wed...

Lightning tossed his hair impatiently. He'd have to keep a rein on himself, so he would, or keen Gypsy eyes would spy out his lust and make merry over how eager he'd been.

"You let it down," Traveler said unexpectedly. Lightning was puzzled for a moment, then felt his soul-mate's fingers running through the shining black locks close to his scalp. "Was this for me?"

Well and well, it *had* been, but Lightning balked at answering outright. He mumbled some things that weren't quite words, to which Traveler laughed outright.

And so, with a blush and with a frolic, they reached the Gypsy encampment.

Packed full of Gypsies, from small children to tottering Grannies, each and every one directing their full attention on Lightning and Traveler.

Oh, no.

"Lightning, is this your doing?" Traveler sounded displeased.

"None of mine," Lightning replied through tight lips. "I meant for this to be a quiet ceremony. Quiet."

"Appears word's gotten out, hasn't it?"

"Ho, the happy couple!" a tall, lanky fellow called loudly enough for all to hear. "Players, give us music! Celebrate!"

Ringed round about the pair, fiddlers and harpers and drummer and pipers began a sprightly dance-tune, throwing heart and soul into their performance. The watching women and children squealed in excitement, turning to their men for a dance.

Lightning peeped at Traveler. Lords, lords, what must he be thinking?

His reaction proved to be a surprise. Traveler's frown transmuted into a broad grin, and he held out one good sturdy hand for Lightning to take. "'Twould be a shame for such good music to go to waste. Will you?"

Without a second thought -- well, save for a tiny one questioning the man's sanity -- Lightning took that hand and let himself be whirled into the dance.

Ah! Unexpected, but such a delight! Caught up in his arms, Lightning fast discovered how Traveler knew his way around the steps of the Gypsy gambols, twirling him with a right good will and a fine skill. Lightning found himself unable to stop smiling broad and bright, reflecting Traveler's good humor turn for turn, nor to calm his bounding excitement.

When the music came to a stop, they spun in one more circle and collapsed in one another's arms, full of mirth. Lightning hadn't had such fun in ages!

In the moment between music and moving on, Traveler stroked Lightning's hair and trailed a finger down the line of his jaw. "You look young as your years," he whispered. "And I find myself glad to be here, to do this with you."

Lightning's lips parted. "As do I," he replied, honest and true, thoughts of duty discarded in favor of joy. His blood sang with the old enchantments, and his body felt every

Faire Grounds

inch filled with vivid life.

This was right. They were meant to be together.

"Now what?" Traveler asked, still quiet.

Lightning placed a hand on his soul-mate's chest and guided him to face forward, to the caravans. "You'll see."

A Granny, the oldest Lightning had ever known, tottered out from behind the crowd, braced on two solid, knotty sticks. She stood hunched nearly in half, but when she craned her neck to look up at the pair of men her gaze was clear as a young girl's. Mischievous, and all-knowing, besides.

"We have come here to ask --" Lightning began.

"Bah, bah." The Granny waved her hand to cut off his words. "I know what you've come a-looking for. As the eldest among this gathered community, the right is mine to grant you what you seek." She looked back and forth between them. Despite his nerves, Lightning refused to be cowed by her sharp stare. From the corner of his eye, he saw Traveler standing tall and proud as well.

"Oh-ho, what a pair you make," the Granny cackled. "You'll have quite the life together, but here's my blessing: may you love as fierce as you're bound to fight, and never go to bed a-angered." She thumped one of her sticks. "Hold out your hands, the pair of you."

Lightning shot out his wrist. Traveler followed suit a little more slowly, as if he were watching and copying, not sure of what to do, but made his way there in the end.

The Granny handed one stick to a woman standing close by, and hobbled toward them. From one rusty black pocket, she drew a red kerchief. "Steady now," she jibed wickedly. "Men, men, they're all the same."

She tied the kerchief around Traveler and Lightning's wrists with surprisingly deft hands, for all they were knotted with age. Resting one palm on the kerchief's knot, she stared at them until they were compelled to look back, Lightning, for one, examining her face.

Grannies often had magic of their own, and it paid to heed their advice if they chose to give any.

She grunted in satisfaction once she had both their attention. "You *will* fight," she pronounced. "But you *will* love, as well. When stormy weather blows, hold fast to the love you know you both feel despite how you were thrust into one another's lives. Hold fast, ne'er let go, and find a happy ending to this chapter of your life's tale."

Before Lightning could interrupt -- perhaps a good thing, for truth, it would have been abominable manners -- although a host of questions rose in his mind -- the Granny stepped back and accepted her second stick. She raised her voice in the clear, bell-like tones of a girl. "It is done! Lightning and Traveler are bound as one. Now celebrate, one and all, celebrate! Music, dancing, feasting and all -- this is a proper Gypsy marriage!"

The musicians struck to with eagerness as the gathered Gypsies burst into excited chattering, the two noises clashing against one

Faire Grounds

another in a wild jamboree of sound.

Lightning should have gone to throw himself in the midst of the crowd, but he lingered to touch Traveler where the kerchief bound them. "Are you well?"

Traveler gazed at Lightning with a heat-filled look. A heat that promised all Lightning had been dreaming about and more, all to come soon as they could be alone. "Very well," he rumbled. "Now, let's not have this revelry be wasted either. 'Tis not what I'd expected..." He paused. "Life with you never will be." He gave Lightning's arse a hard *thwack* with his free hand. "Now, do as we've been bidden. Celebrate!"

"Aye." Lightning let more than a touch of his own hunger show in his tone and the way he returned Traveler's stare. "But I'll look forward to our own frolics later, more than these."

"Lad," Traveler murmured in the way that reduced Lightning to a quivering mass of need every time, "know this for sure." He bent to kiss Lightning, licking a heated trail across his lips. "You're in for the night of your life."

Lightning bubbled up with laughter. Lords of the Road, he surely hoped so!

Chapter Nine

Say what one might about them, but more so than any other race of folk, Gypsies knew how to celebrate. The musicians never ceased their playing, racing from one tune to the next with nary a pause. Dancers spun in circles among children chasing to and fro, not colliding nor misstepping once. All, when the urge fell upon them, made their way to the boiling stewpots and campfires where only the best and most savory treats were to be found in abundance.

The only thing they lacked were sweets, as those were too dear for even a handfasting, but as the evening rolled on, Lightning found himself face-to-face with Nell. Wild red curls, free of any net, whipped willy-nilly around her pale Grounder face. She stood out like a beacon on the dark sea, but didn't look as if she cared two copper bits.

"For all that it's your own special day; you're a hard man to catch hold of!" Nell took Lightning by the forearms, familiar as ever, beaming at him as she might at her own son on his wedding day, had she any children.

Lightning supposed he stood as proxy for the grooms of her own line she'd never get to

Faire Grounds

chivvy, and so he kept his patience. Not so very hard a task; he liked Nell, after all, despite -- or because of -- her ways, Grounder or no.

Aye, and will I be a Grounder soon, myself? A deserter of the road? Surely not; not when the caravan gleams ever brighter than before with my duty done? Perhaps Traveler will feel the call of the road again.

I can but hope, though, eh?

"Woolgathering," Nell said with a *tsk*. She dimpled wickedly. "Dreaming about your wedding night, were you?"

Lightning blushed to the tips of his ears.

Nell pounced. "You were, then. Mercy, not as I can blame you. Your Traveler's handsome enough to make me wish I'd had a chance at his hand." She fanned herself. "I'd say you made a good choice, based on his looks alone."

Traveler? Handsome? The thought had, oddly, never occurred to Lightning before. He turned about to search for his mate and found him at one of the cooking-fires, tasting someone's no-doubt prized recipe. He laughed and tilted his head back, giving Lightning a good look at the man in the firelight.

Lords of the Road. Why did I never...? He'd been blind, and that was a fact. Traveler's face wasn't the standard idol of masculine good looks, interesting and full of character instead. The uncharitable would call him plain as Slipstream, but only if they failed to see the force of personality that transformed him into something fascinating and all the more appealing. Short hair, oddly short for a Gypsy, although the close crop suited him well. And his body...Lightning swallowed, feeling his cheeks grow warmer. Traveler had a body made not just for pleasure, but hard work. Broad and strong, narrow at the waist, solid in the leg.

"Handsome," Lightning echoed dumbly. "Aye...he is."

"Do not tease our young friend so, Nell." Meilin appeared from nowhere to place his honey-colored hand on Nell's shoulder. "He is too innocent for your jokes."

Nell bridled saucily. "Innocent, eh? Then why's he got a guilty look about his eyes when I speak about his wedding night?"

"If he has dipped into the well a bit early, where is the harm?" Meilin folded his hands into his sleeves. "Leave well enough alone."

"Oh, naughty, naughty. Then you won't be needing any lessons on how to satisfy a man in bed, will you?"

Lightning's jaw hardened. "I swore to virginity until I found my life-mate. I kept that vow."

"Just so." Meilin nodded. "My best wishes to you, young Lightning, and to your husband. Blessings as well, which are not lightly given among my people. In times of trouble, if I am close by, come to me and I will guide you as best I can."

Humbled, Lightning bowed from the waist. "Many thanks, and if I may ever return the favor, come to me."

"I would not say no to some tea. I lack the coin, but back where I come from we drink it every day."

"I'll see you get a goodly supply, and soon."

"A fine bargain and well made." Meilin gave a crisp nod. "Nell, we had best be on our way."

"He's after dragging me back to the Grounders' part of the faire before we're spotted missing," Nell groused. "If we must, we must. Oh! Here, Lightning. I almost forgot. Open your hands." When he did, she pressed a warm bundle wrapped in white cloth on him. "Sweet honey cakes for your wedding breakfast. See, see, I know a little Gypsy lore." She twinkled at him. "But mind you, even if you're up all the night long, don't sleep through the next day!"

Lightning flushed again.

"Nell," Meilin said crisply, apparently deciding she needed a literal firm hand, one at her elbow, to guide her away. "Fare you well, Lightning."

"Fare you well." Lightning watched as Nell and Meilin made their way through the crowds, Meilin without a hitch but many a stop to drag Nell away from the lure of a cooking-pot or a circle of youths dancing to a sprightly jig.

The bundle Nell had given him smelled sweet and fragrant, and its warmth told him she'd made these special for his nuptial day. He found himself amused...and oddly touched.

"Who were they?"

Lightning glanced up to see Traveler at his side, looking a bit worse for wear after a day's rambunctious revelry, but still sharp and aye, now he'd seen for himself, so very handsome in his way. "The Grounder and her companion? My friends."

"You have friends?"

"Is that so hard to believe?"

"I have learned, Lightning, to ever and ever expect the unexpected with you." Traveler tousled Lightning's hair, then leaned in to steal a quick kiss.

Their lips lingered, that kiss drawing out in a slow, sweet tasting of one another's mouths. Lightning could sense a sudden building urgency in Traveler's touch, and knew Traveler would feel the same in him.

When they parted, Traveler took Lightning by the arm. "Will anyone be offended if we go?" he whispered.

Lightning shook his head. "I shouldn't wonder they're surprised we haven't already gone."

"Imp! To tell me we could have been away long before now?"

"You looked as if you were having such a fine time..."

Traveler tapped Lightning's nose. "Think you're clever, do you? I'll just add another lesson on the list of things I mean to teach you."

Lightning shivered with pleasure at the sound of that, aye, he did. He knew from delicious experience just how Traveler tended to get his point across...and what point he used, in truth. "Do you threaten or promise?"

"Both." Traveler glittered at him. "Down to the shore, Lightning, and now. I'll spend this wedding-night on my island and not in your caravan where anyone might get a free show."

It went against custom of consummating a union in the home on wheels, but he'd been hoping Traveler would choose to take him back to his house on the sea. Revelry and frolic were fine in their place, but after a day of such riotous jubilation, Lightning's head ached. "I go with you," he said, letting Traveler take his hand and lead him along.

Giving Traveler the reins felt right.

* * *

And here I am, a married man. I've no clue what to do next -- well, nay, I know what comes next -- but afterwards? There's so much at risk for the both of us. I'd not keep Lightning from the road, yet I'll not journey again myself.

Welladay, I'll think on it tomorrow, he promised himself.

Another thought tapped him on the shoulder, one he'd pushed to the back of his mind when it first was born, and tried to keep well hidden there. *What if he finds out you're not a Gypsy for true? He will, you know. Some of the Lords don't like for a man to be too happy, and there's a fact. Unless you're very, very lucky or very, very careful, he'll figure out the truth. And for a Gypsy who puts so much stock in honesty, above all things honesty...and even beyond the deception, even with the enchantment, would he willingly tie himself to a man born and raised a Grounder?*

Traveler ground his teeth. *I'll figure out a way to keep him in the dark, for his own protection. For mine. He's worked his way into my heart, and I will not lose my flash of Lightning now we're bound one unto the other.*

It'll be all right. I'll make it be all right, and bedamned to anything that suggests I might not be able.

"Traveler?" Lightning asked, unusually subdued. Traveler looked down at his lean Gypsy youth, truly his own now, and noted as how he bore an expression of worry. "You look darksome as a storm. What ails?"

Ah, and he cut to the chase quick as ever, didn't he? "Nothing," Traveler lied, regretting the falsehood.

One now. There will be more. They'll mount and mount until there's a hill you cannot climb -- and then, then they'll come crashing down about your ears.

"Forgive me, Lightning," he sighed. He ground the balls of his hands into his eyes and groaned softly. "I am tired. Very tired. It has been a day longer than any I can remember."

Lightning looked stricken. "Do you regret this, then?"

"Regret? No, not at all. And I would do it again, if you asked," he said, turning to look up at the sky, at the stars. "Again and again if such would please you."

Lightning shook his head, clearly baffled. "Then why do you seem so troubled?"

Do not ask me that question. I have no answers ready you would care to hear.

Traveler forced a friendly smile. "I bide too

Faire Grounds

much by myself, that's my trouble. It'll be well to get back home. Nothing else to concern yourself with."

"You're certain?" Lightning didn't look any too convinced.

"I am. Ah, here, the boat." Traveler spied his craft with relief and made quick tracks, jumping in with the skill born of long habit. "Do you need a hand?"

"I need it not, but I'll take what you offer." Lightning's tone held a subtle nuance, a well-laced double meaning setting Traveler's cock on the rise.

To hells with what the morrow brought. They'd have a night not to be forgotten first.

Though the hour had grown near to dark and Traveler misliked rowing during gathering dusk, their sail back to his island went smooth as glass. Lightning sat demurely in his end of the boat, hands folded in his lap while the wind caught his marvelous hair and whirled the locks about.

Truth, Traveler was half-surprised he hadn't crashed purely from distraction at the sight of his beautiful boy.

Luck came leaping off the gate to greet the pair of them as they walked up Traveler's yard. He meowed insistently, unmistakably scolding both in turn.

"Here, now, you shouldn't tie your fur in knots over my leaving for a time," Traveler chided. "I've brought Lightning. You remember him, eh?"

Luck gave Traveler his perfected *"you fool"* look before tripping his way over to wind around Lightning's legs. He purred like a lion, making Lightning chuckle. "Good lad."

"Will someone see to Patpaw's needs?" Traveler found himself glad of the excuse to make small talk, as the silence they'd fallen into on the boat seemed to linger, sealing his mouth against things he would have said -- a welcome to his home, now their home, for one. The quiet felt almost tangible to boot, keeping him from whirling Lightning out of the boat and directly into a hungry kiss.

"I laid out a bowl of good fresh water, and she'll no doubt beg around fire after fire until she's plump as a tick on things she knows better than to eat. She should be fine." Lightning shuffled his feet and tilted his head at Traveler. "This is...awkward, isn't it?"

"Aye. Though I don't ken why it should be. Do you?"

Lightning raised his shoulders. "The stories don't say anything about wedding nights. Horsetail and Slipstream, my fathers, always told me I was too young to hear about such things, but they died before they deemed me old enough."

Traveler felt a twinge of pity. "How old were you when they passed, lad?"

"Twelve." Lightning's jaw jutted out. "I got by."

Twelve. Lords of the Road, but he's made of sturdy stuff. "You never cease to amaze me," Traveler murmured, the uneasiness dropping away as would a discarded cloak. "Come here, beloved."

He could see the same easiness settle on

Faire Grounds

Lightning's muscles. The lad rolled his shoulders, then smiled -- a bit shyly -- and walked forward into Traveler's waiting arms.

They held one another for a long moment, Lightning's face nestled against Traveler's chest, arms wound around one another's backs, the rushing sound of the sea and the smell of salt filling their other senses.

So precious to me already, Traveler marveled. *Does he know? And am I half so dear to him?*

Out loud, he said, "Up to the house, Lightning. The lawn's a fine soft grass, but I've a mind to spend my wedding night in a proper bed."

Lightning's eyes widened. He nodded. And when they parted from their embrace, he clung to Traveler's hand. "Follow me," Traveler soothed. "I'll lead you right."

Or he would do his best, so he would.

"I have and will put my trust in you." Lightning stood on tiptoe and pressed his lips to the angle of Traveler's jawbone. "Thank you."

His breath caught in his throat as Lightning's words plucked at the deep guilt within. "Beloved..."

"Yes. As you are mine."

Traveler reached out to tangle his fingers in Lightning's hair. "You are a wonder when your quills are down."

"I'm no porcupine."

"Aye, but you are. Just as the finest of roses have their thorns, you will always have your prickles, Lightning, and I would not love you half so well without them. Never change, little thorn."

"Then I remain as I am, and please the both of us at once."

The mood had grown somber again. In an effort to stave off another floundering silence, he tugged lightly at a rogue strand of hair plastered against Lightning's cheek. "After our sail, you look as if you have been dragged through a holly bush backwards."

Lightning pulled away, but with a laugh. "If I leave it down for you as you like, you'll see me in like disarray more than often."

"I do have my preference for seeing you unbound." Traveler recalled a bit of old-fashioned Gypsy lore, put two and two together, and came up with the reason behind Lightning's lengthy mane. "May you never know such pain or loss that you feel the need to cut your hair in mourning, my thorn."

"Your own hair is short," Lightning ventured.

Traveler hid his wince as yet another lie sprang to his lips. "We all have our sorrows."

"If I could take them away, I would." Lightning vowed in deadly earnest even as he clasped at Traveler's hand in his hair.

"I think you would, Lightning. I can see you charging back into the shadowy deeps of my misery, sword in your teeth, ready to challenge anyone to fight over the fate of a scruffy boy's soul." He squeezed Lightning's fingers gently. "For that I thank you, my own."

That, more than anything, seemed to

please Lightning until he glowed.

Traveler's patience began to wear thin. "Inside?" he suggested.

"Oh, aye," Lightning agreed eagerly. "Inside."

* * *

Though they stopped for many a kiss along the way, Traveler managed to lead Lightning in the right direction, into the room where he was accustomed to taking his rest. Alone.

Not alone tonight.

With Lightning twined in his arms, Traveler could but groan with pleasure. He buried both hands in Lightning's hair, running his fingers through the treasure with growing delight. His cock was stiff enough to ache, and at the notion of winding Lightning's hair around the length, it gave a mighty jump. "So beautiful," he swore. "So wonderful. Lightning..."

The excitement never dulled no matter how many times their lips touched. Traveler leaned forward and pressed his mouth to Lightning's. The kiss began in a fit of passion and strength that could make a man crumble to his knees and climb back up for more. Lightning's arms were somehow around Traveler's neck, and his encircling Lightning's back.

"The bed is not far," Traveler mumbled against Lightning's mouth.

"Is it not, then?" Lightning tore away with a look of glee more suited to his years than his usual somber mien. "I'll race you there."

"Oh, you will, will you?"

Laughing and scrambling, they tussled their way onto the raised dais covered in sheepskins, Lightning landing among the softness a half-second before Traveler did. "I won," he informed Traveler, stretching luxuriously into the soft, wooly pelts.

"So you did." Traveler tilted to the right in curiosity. "What do I pay as forfeit?"

Lightning glanced about himself. "Oh...you have...and so many...light the candles."

"To please you, aye." They were enchanted candles, each with a spell laid on its wax to keep it ever-burning, but Traveler planned on keeping Lightning far too distracted to notice anything odd. He raised himself with reluctance, moved in great haste, and completed his task in record time.

Once lit, the candles filled Traveler's sleeping chamber with a soft glow. "Between the sheepskins and this fragrant light, one might think you were trying to seduce me," Lightning teased. He lifted one leg to plant his foot flat on the bed, deliberately tempting Traveler with a hint of things to come. "Is that your plan, then?"

"Not plan. Intention."

Lightning's lips curved in a lazy smile. He dropped one hand over the side of the dais.

Both heard the sound of crinkling paper.

Damnation! "Lightning, leave that be," Traveler ordered.

"Why?" The prickles flared back up as Lightning snatched the scrap of parchment, then quilled in puzzlement as he gazed on what

Faire Grounds

he saw there. "This is...this is me. Where did you get such a thing?"

Traveler considered yet another lie, but the words stuck in his throat and after a moment he confessed, "I drew this myself."

"Truly?" Lightning lightly traced his own features. "I've no skill for art, though I'd often longed to paint and draw."

"Perhaps I'll teach you how, by and bye." He hesitated. "And if you like this...there is another."

One he'd done from memory and kept well-hidden, not half so careless as with the first sketch.

"Let me see," Lightning demanded immediately, sitting up and stretching out his hand.

"Then sit up, for you're lying on the paper. Just beneath the pillow, tucked between bed's-edge and wall." He watched as Lightning fished around for his drawing, and waited keenly for his response to what he'd see.

* * *

His husband could draw? Wonder upon wonders. Lightning's hand closed on the hidden scrap of paper and drew it out, holding the sketch up to the candlelight to better see.

He saw, and gaped at the lush charcoal lines. He looked real as life in Traveler's rendition. Perhaps a little too real! "Traveler," he breathed. "How did you...?"

Traveler had drawn him asleep and nude, curled up like a wood-elf amongst a bed of furs.

The faintest suggestion of wings emerged from his back. Just behind his likeness, Lightning saw a shape -- a vagueness of light and shadow that might or might not have been a man bending over his vulnerable body.

"Do you not like it?" Traveler asked him gravely. "Tell me, Lightning. Does my drawing offend? The shadow behind you, are you glad to see it or do you wish for more light to chase it away? Tell me! I must...I must know." He held out a beautiful, perfect hand for him to take. "Please."

"No," Lightning whispered roughly. "I like it. Traveler..."

He cast the sketch aside, heedless of where it fell, and opened his arms for Traveler. With a low, triumphant chuckle, Traveler rolled into them, his chest against Lightning's own.

For a moment, Lightning heard nothing but their breathing.

"I have drawn us thus," Traveler rasped, his words warm against the cool curve of Lightning's neck. He kissed him beneath the angle of his chin.

A fine shivering ran through Lightning like the fluttering of those wings Traveler had drawn.

"I have drawn us many times this past three days and night," Traveler murmured against the hollow of Lightning's neck. "Would you like to hear this, Prickles? Shall I tell you of how I have sketched with useless soft lead a dream that I have burned to make come true?"

Lightning curled tighter against his mate, hungry for the man's all-encompassing warmth. "Tell me," he ordered.

Traveler stroked the bare flesh of Lightning's collarbone, so near and yet so far from his nipples, tingling and aching for want of his touch, aye, more than anything in the world. "I have drawn us on the soft feather-stuffed pillows before the sketching room firepit," he whispered. "There is nothing between us, not even a wisp of silk –- just your sweet flesh against my own. Our arms and legs are tangled together...just so, like this...and there is a glimpse of your face over my shoulder, rising like a swan above your neck arched with passion –- wanting me so much as I want you. Lightning -- *my* Lightning --"

He burrowed his face into Lightning's neck and pulled him closer than ever before. Lightning's body molded to the planes of Traveler's, feeling the evidence of the man's desire pressed hot and hard against the curve of his own hip.

Traveler groaned, digging his fingers into Lightning's hair like a drowning man seeking a lifeline. Lightning lifted his face to hungrily devour Traveler's kiss. "Lightning," he said in voiced wonder, "Do you know now what you do to me?"

Lightning's head swam, dizzied with the sweet scent of candles and the scorching heat of Traveler's body. He discovered he was roaming over Traveler's chest, stroking the hard muscles with the tips of his fingers. The tortured growl that his touch pulled from Traveler gave him a deep, rich thrill of triumph better than reaching the top of a mountain peak.

Gladly did Lightning arch against his mate, a soft moan that might have been "yes" escaping his lips. Traveler buried his answering groan on the skin of Lightning's chest, fingers pinching Lightning's nipples exactly as he'd wanted, but not known how to request.

Good -- so good -- but not enough. "Harder," Lightning demanded, covering Traveler's hands with his own. "I'm not a flower."

"As my beloved, declares it, then let it be so."

"Good," he said breathlessly. Without waiting, his fingers scrabbled at the unyielding canvas of Traveler's trews. "Off!"

He gave a full-throated, delighted laugh. "Lightning, there is no one like you in the wide world!"

"There had best never be, either. Ever."

"Never, when there is you, so warm and alive in my arms." He raised a finger to Lightning's lips. "I know, I know. 'Get on with it'. And so I will."

Traveler lowered his mouth to Lightning's own, seeking and devouring hungrily as between them they writhed and wiggled their wedding clothes off and cast them far aside, out of the way.

Lightning approved, stroking the hard curve of Traveler's arse to let him know as much. His cock rubbed against Lightning's, the friction even better than Traveler's harsh nipple-play, and yet not enough.

He knew what would be -- and he was ready.

"Traveler?"

"Lightning?" Traveler examined Lightning's face. He groaned, almost a growl. "Yes. Yes, at last. Oil. We'll need oil."

"We do not." Lightning lifted his legs to wrap them around Traveler's back. "Touch me and see," he said softly. "I've been ready for you all the day long."

Traveler did test to see, and shook his head in wonder. "No one like you," he echoed, then murmured something that sounded like a devoutly thankful prayer. With one swift plunge, he buried the length of himself inside Lightning, tightly sheathed, deep as he could possibly go.

Lightning raised his voice in a cry of mixed pain and ecstasy, and then in an ululating Gypsy howl of triumph.

The sound of his own wedding-cry undid Lightning completely. He lost himself inside the cloud that rose to engulf his mind, knowing nothing but the thrusting weight of Traveler's cock, the heat and the light and the musky smell of Traveler's skin.

Mine, my own, my beloved, my mate, he repeated over and over again, hearing his own name chanted as they rose higher and higher together, past the very skies...and into the white-hot burst of the sun.

"Jasha," Lightning heard hissed amongst their noises of passion. *"Jasha!"*

The voice sounded as if it came from someone else's throat. Lightning fought to hold still. "Traveler, who calls?"

Traveler shook his head. "No one. No one,

beloved." He resumed his eager fucking, the thrusting of his cock and the hot rain of his kisses soon driving all thoughts of anything else from Lightning's mind until they came one after another in a mighty, dazzling explosion of seed and bliss.

Although Lightning would recall, some time later, how in the midst of their consummation bliss a voice had accused Traveler in an almost-forgotten tongue:

"Traitor..."

Chapter Ten

Is this love? What is love? Is it a little more than fondness when you mix fondness with passion and lust? I feel sure I'm in love with my Lightning, but...what does such a thing mean?

Uneasy, Traveler tossed and turned upon his dais-bed. He found himself caught in the twilight realms between sleeping and waking, where he knew he hung on to fragments of dreams but that they were *only* dreams. Lightning, who'd started their rest off wrapped around him sweet as you please, had long since drawn away on the other side of Traveler's bed and curled up in a ball.

Lightning, Traveler thought vaguely, had a bad habit indeed of stealing the covers.

As Traveler flopped over on a side facing the lad, Lightning grumbled in complaint and tugged the blankets tighter around his slim body. Traveler felt the chill of the early morning ocean air, an uncomfortable coldness as their fire had gone out while they slept, but he hadn't the heart to wrestle back an equal portion of the coverings and chance waking his beloved.

Beloved. Love. I thought I knew what love

was, once...

"Love," he recalled a dry old tutor from his youth saying through thin, gray lips, "love is a symptom of a man's needs, those needs which make him weak. A man must take a wife and father heirs, true, but to love her undermines his power. A true man cannot afford the weakness of being fond, for foolish decisions are made when one cares more for a person than for law and justice. Wars have been fought over love, and love has been the key to many a man's damnation. Are you paying attention, Janos?" The elderly man had narrowed no-color eyes at him and scowled. "Mark my words, young prince. You've too much of the romantic about you, and such shall be your downfall if you have not learned to guard against *love*."

Traveler punched his pillow in frustration. He could see his old tutor's point, yes, and of a truth his weakness for Lightning -- enchantments aside -- had put him in great danger, aye. How great the danger he wasn't sure yet, but there came a cold and clammy feeling in his guts when he forgot himself and thought about their future.

A Gypsy of the Road and a man bound to land. How will we solve this?

Answers came no easier to him in the bed this morning than they had before. Traveler exhaled through his nose and chanced reaching out to stroke down Lightning's back, bared to him through fallen blankets. Skin soft as silk, aye, silky as that which covered a cock.

He'd been desperate enough to fuck

Faire Grounds

Lightning that he'd given into the impulse -- weakness? -- to have a taste in the caravan that afternoon not long since. He'd had the youth three times the night before, yet he craved more.

Love. What is it? I must know.

Those who had taught him magic differed in their opinions, although none scorned it as a concept. Some simply couldn't be bothered, some were content to live alone, and yet some had wives or husbands and even children.

One such lady, a woman of great power, had spoken to Traveler once after observing him in a fit of gloom over Rosalind:

"Love is what happens when you find yourself attached to another person in a way you can't properly explain, no. You only know she, or he in your case, brings a warmth to your heart and a light to your eyes. Kisses and embraces and, aye, more, all come naturally as the bond deepens. You begin to care for this person above yourself, when it's good love and pure, and their joys or troubles become your own. The thought of living without them causes you pain, and so you do all in your power to remain by their side. Love makes us more than we once were, for where were one, now we are part of two. There. That's love, my friend."

I can't help but think they were both in the right. Love is a two-sided coin. Makes you weak, makes you strong. You give up part of yourself and get something from another to fill you back up.

I am fond of him, and always have been

since first we met.
Do I love Lightning now, then?
Yes. Of a certainty, yes.

Lightning murmured something not quite words and shifted, a hand coming up beside his face. His palm showed the results of years of hard work, young though he might be. Tough, the Gypsy youth was, and not afraid of plunging in deep waters not knowing if he should sink or swim. A bold, brave lad.

Admiration, too, perhaps that's part of love, but is it a start to the tune or a descant descending?

Love. Pride in his proud young spirit, his stubborn determination. Lust for his strong young body, the kind I have always favored over big solid brutes like myself. Passion that flares bright between us when we come together and make...love. Hah!

Love.

Traveler moved to Lightning's shoulder and gave him a light shake. "Ho, there. Be you awake?"

"As if I could yet be asleep, with the way you toss and turn," Lightning grumbled. His snappish words were belied when he flipped over to face Traveler, for he had a soft, languorous smile on his lips, and a gentle warmth in his gaze. "Good morning, husband."

Traveler chuckled. He began stroking Lightning's hair, still loose, although mercy, but how it had tangled and snarled in his sleep. No matter; he loved the long black locks all the same. *Love.* "You are a wicked scamp," he said in admiration. "The simplest morning greeting and you make me think of wicked things."

"Mmm." Lightning stretched like a cat, casual and sly. "Do I really? What sort of wickedness do I inspire? Which responds, the body or the mind?"

"Both, in equal parts. Come and kiss me, Lightning."

Lightning obeyed, wriggling toward Traveler until they touched chest-to-chest. Even after a night's sleep his breath was fresh and underneath the smells of sex, semen and sweat he had a fresh spice to his scent, tempting Traveler to taste him again.

They kissed, long and sweet, deep and with gathering hunger. Once begun, Traveler could not find it in him to stop. He might have kept on kissing for hours in the lazy dawn, idly stroking his Gypsy lad wherever his hands chanced to light, but Lightning drew away, sparkling with wickedness. "Is a kiss all you ask of me?"

Bedamned to questions and doubts. While I have him, I will enjoy him.

Traveler rolled Lightning onto his back and rose up over him. The lad's cock was stiff, as was his own of a normal morning, but they could put the wood to good use and build a fine bright fire. "Not all," he murmured, rocking against Lightning so their pricks rubbed together.

Lightning threw his head back in pleasure. Traveler gazed at him in appreciation. He loved -- aye, *loved* -- the look on Lightning's face when he discovered a new joy. Throat tilted, lips fallen apart in pleasure, and eyes closed.

For howsoever long this lasted, and Traveler found himself hoping it would for always and ever, that they *would* find a solution to their problems and an escape from danger, he would spend as many waking moments as he could devising a way to bring that look of wanton abandon to his Lightning-love's face.

And gathering Lightning in his arms, Traveler began to stroke hard against the lad's stomach, sure their cocks rubbed firm side by side, showing him how one of the simplest ways of joining could be good as any other.

* * *

"You call this a bath?" Lightning stood at the edge of Traveler's hand-constructed pool, eyeing the rocks that guided gentle waves in and out of a rough-hewn tub on the shore.

"What would be wrong with this?" Traveler splashed Lightning, feeling playful.

"It's *salt*," Lightning pointed out. "Salt water is bad as no water for cleansing a body." He shuddered. "I'd come out crusty as a codfish and feel like a walking deer-lick."

"Ah, picky, picky. Cease your complaining and come on in." Traveler swam to the side of the pool and tugged with one wet hand at Lightning's ankle. Lightning swore and shouted as he lost his balance, finally forced to the only choice of toppling forward into the water.

He surfaced spluttering and angry as Luck might be if he'd fallen in Lightning's place. Dragging heavy hanks of hair out of his face, he glared at Traveler. "I suppose you think you're funny, aye?"

"How else was I to get you in here but to manhandle you about?" Traveler had begun to be able to tell, a little, when Lightning was upset for true, and when he bristled out of habit but no malice. "There. You're in, now. Tell me what you think of my 'salt' pool."

Lightning scowled, but to give the lad credit he tested to see for himself before he rendered any judgment. He wandered forward, feeling his way across slick, moss-covered stones.

As for Traveler, well, he enjoyed a good eyeful of Lightning's naked arse as the youth explored.

When Lightning turned, Traveler had himself another fine eyeful of Lightning's delightful cock, too. Soft now, but capable of great feats when you teased it up proper-like. "The water's soft. Warm. How? The oceans are freezing, even during this time of year."

A bit of magic, of course, a treat for Lightning -- normally Traveler *did* take his baths cold and salty. He shrugged and waved a hand. "The warmth comes of the moss on the stones," he fibbed. "They generate heat for to make the temperature mild. As for soft, well, blame the moss as well. 'Tis a wondrous thing, and I'm careful of its growth as any Grounder of their hothouse roses."

Lie upon lie upon lie. Traveler willed himself not to look guiltily aside.

Lightning prodded the moss with a toe, just visible as a ripple of moving flesh through the water. "Why do you not sell this? You'd fetch a fine price. Many a Gypsy on the move or one of the Road-kin would kill for warm baths."

"The thought never occurred to me. Perhaps I will, now, or I'll make gifts." Traveler had no intention of doing any such thing, as the whole story was a cobble of lies, but he found himself too eager for Lightning's approval to curse himself -- much -- for spinning these yarns.

Time to think later, to regret later, to riddle out solutions later.

Now, we enjoy one another.

Lightning tasted the water. "Only mildly salty," he said in surprise. "No more than mineral baths I've tried. Is this a virtue of the moss, too?"

"Aye. Sit yourself down on the ledge -- you'll see stones arranged in a sort of seat below water's level -- and let me look at you."

"Look at me?" Lightning sounded surprised, then amused. "What would you see? I am as I am. A Gypsy covered in seed and perspiration, his hair a-tangle as an elf-knotted horse's mane."

"Nay. You are more. You are mine."

As Traveler began making his way across the pool, intent forming solidly in his mind, Lightning's lips curved in a new-learned knowing and anticipation. "Again? You're lustier than I'd suspect, if you'd know the truth."

"And you love me for it." Traveler reached Lightning and scooped him up, holding the lad in both arms, letting him float in the water. The smooth side of his mate's neck called to him, demanding kisses and tasting.

Why should he not give in to what he craved? Traveler buried his face against Lightning's throat and began suckling up yet more love-marks to add to his collection.

Lightning hummed with enjoyment as Traveler used his mouth till he'd been satisfied -- for the time being. He looked languid and sleepy yet still impish as he met Traveler gaze-to-gaze. "Do you have a new game?"

His fine tenor was all the better for a newly-learned purr of sexual hunger.

"I do. I would be inside you again, Lightning." Traveler slipped beneath Lightning's arse to touch the soft skin, then slide a finger between the cheeks. Recklessly using magic as he pleased, he eased away any soreness of muscle or entrance.

"Oh!" Lightning gasped. "I should be used to this by now, shouldn't I?"

"'Tis one of the virtues of sex. Never gets old, it doesn't." Traveler chucked Lightning's chin with his free hand. "Touch me. Feel how hard I am for you? All for you." He hissed as Lightning unerringly found and circled his cock, squeezing in a way the canny lad had already figured Traveler enjoyed. "And are you, for me?"

"Aye. I'd think myself bespelled -- well, I suppose I am; there's the enchantment after all -- but I'll trust in what you say, and speak the truth. I burn for you."

"Then let's see what we can do with a proper fire." Lightning hadn't washed; he would yet be slick with the oils they'd used the night before, aye, and with spilled seed besides. As Traveler pushed at his pucker with two fingers, the lad relaxed for him straight away. Still tight enough to please the most particular, but there'd be no pain for Lightning, only pleasure. "Clever lad," Traveler approved.

"I had a good teacher."

"So you did. Now make your tutor proud. Here I sit, and here you sit facing me. What would you do now, do you think?"

Ah, but how cunning Lightning became in a twinkle. "Just this," he said simply, using nimble legs to shift forward and with uncanny instinct, lowered himself onto Traveler's aching shaft. He sank down with a hiss of delight as he was impaled, not stopping until his arse rested flush with Traveler's groin. "Aye?"

"Aye," Traveler forced around his swelling excitement. Not only could Lightning take his breath away, he could steal his words.

"Like a horse," Lightning said. "I ride."

He lifted himself a few tantalizing inches, then lowered once again. He purred with amusement at Traveler's groan, then voiced a moan himself and began to fuck and be fucked in earnest.

Traveler grabbed Lightning's waist and held on tight as the youth moved. Up and down, up and down, muscles squeezing and heat incredible. They began to breathe harshly, panting for air as their hearts beat faster and bodies flushed with excitement.

"Good?" Traveler found breath to ask, thrusting up in his turn and seizing Lightning's stiff cock with deep appreciation and appetite.

That cock answered for him, jerking upward, but Lightning replied all the same, his breath nigh gone, "Good!"

"Harder."

"Aye. Harder."

The water churned around the pair of them as Traveler lost himself in the white-hot glory of fucking -- no, making *love,* love as he'd had such deep thoughts of earlier.

When Lightning came, spilling hot seed over Traveler's hand under the water, he leaned so far that only Traveler's grip kept him from tipping over backwards. The yank at his embedded cock ought to have been painful, but the twist drove Traveler past his limits, shooting seed deep into Lightning's arse.

The two hung together for a long moment, and then began laughing.

And oh, but the laughing felt good.

* * *

"I should be going back," Lightning said, much to Traveler's dismay. They'd washed each other off after a bit and a bit, then come out to flop down on Traveler's lawn, not ashamed a whit for their nudity while they dried. Who was to see?

"Back so soon?"

"I've wares to sell. The Gypsy-kin will look

after my goods, but I should be doing business -- ah, stop that with your hand." Lightning swatted Traveler away from his bare stomach. "I come to faires like this and put up with all the rubbish for the sake of earning enough coin to see me through the winter."

Has he thought of biding here with me during the season of snows? Lords of the Road, does he expect me to be at his side?

Or has he thought about these matters at all?

Traveler didn't ask, for he didn't yet want to know.

He didn't offer his own coin -- bound or no, Lightning's pride would likely make him refuse -- though he could well have afforded the whole stock of tea his Gypsy carried.

Aye, and where had he gone to find such riches? How had he come by so much? Lightning would rather die than be dishonest, Traveler felt certain, yet he knew even he couldn't gather so great a quantity of tea leaves without a mighty feat of magic.

Admiration, he thought again.

I must not lose him. I'll do what I must.

"Lie still, on your back, just as you are," Traveler said hoarsely, getting up on his knees. "Spread your legs, Lightning-my-Lightning. Let me between your thighs."

"And you are not yet satisfied."

"Don't try and fool me into thinking you don't want this, lad."

"I never claimed any such, did I?" Lightning parted his limbs, sprawling wide open, a lazy smile on his face. His prick, young and vigorous, was already beginning to swell nicely, aye, very nicely.

Traveler forgot about the chance of being recognized as a phantom mouth and hurried between Lightning's legs. He hunkered down into a good position, reached for Lightning's cock, and without any words drew the organ into his mouth and began to suck and use his tongue.

Lightning reached for the sky and keened out his ecstasy.

* * *

"And what do you think you're doing now? I'm busy making us a meal. *You* might have a belly full of spendings, but some of us are hungry."

"To hells with eating," Traveler crooned, embracing Lightning tight from behind as the Gypsy made free with Traveler's stock of bread and cheese. "I'd not say no to your tasting the sort of thing I've filled myself with, though."

"Oh, aye, wouldn't you? I'll keep the thought in mind. But now, I eat."

Lightning raised a makeshift sandwich to his mouth and tore off a bite with strong white teeth. He groaned in pleasure at the tastes and textures of Traveler's preferred cheese, smooth as cream, and the bread, enchanted to stay fresh as if it had just come from an oven.

To his credit, Traveler waited until Lightning had swallowed his bite, lest he choke, before he tackled Lightning to the floor.

Lightning tried his best to look stern after they'd rolled and wrestled to a halt. His cock pressed hard against Traveler's stomach even as he scolded, "And what do you think you might be doing? I'm *hungry.*"

"Aye? Well, then, I'll fill you," Traveler murmured, moving to prod at Lightning's entrance yet again. "Fill you till you're bursting."

The orgasms they shared were no less sweet for being had on the cold stone pantry floor, their thrusts no less urgent nor their kisses anything but ravenous.

Lightning, Lightning, this must *be love. I cannot get enough of you...*

Traveler had, completely, forgotten about enchantments -- save for when he spent his own magic to please the Gypsy.

Yet even then, he forgot about the prices men must pay for being such a care-for-naught spendthrift...

* * *

Lightning sat up in the dais bed while Traveler re-lit his candles. "When did you put new tapers in the sconces?"

"While you slept," Traveler lied. "You're not doing as I told you, now, are you? Lie back and look at the ceiling."

It was a mark of how far Lightning's prickles had softened that he did as directed, folding his hands over his chest.

Sex hung in the air -- memories of seed spent hours before, blissful soreness from

Faire Grounds

having fucked the day away, and thrumming anticipation of what was still to come. Sex filled Traveler's bedroom like a living thing, a coiling snake bewitching the pair of them with its unblinking stare.

Had he in his right mind, Traveler later realized, he might have sensed or even seen those snake eyes. But at the moment, all and all of his attention was focused on Lightning and Lightning alone.

After finishing his circuit with tinderbox and candles, Traveler walked to one of the carven chests scattered through his sleeping chamber. If memory served him aright..."No peeking, now," he warned as he opened the lid. "Be a good lad."

"I'm always good for you." Lightning's voice was husky, knowing exactly how much power he had over Traveler and reveling in it.

To his satisfaction, Traveler found what he sought in the chest. Gathering up a handful of buttery-soft leather straps, a peacock feather, and a long, thick phallus, well-polished, carved of smooth marble, all touched by magic and paid for with a high price of blood as well as coin, he took no second thoughts before heading toward his bed with the treasure trove.

Lightning arched an eyebrow. "You have some plan for these?"

"Aye, and you'll enjoy yourself, you will."

"I've never seen the like before." Lightning frowned at the tangle of straps. "What purpose do they serve?"

Traveler roared with lust-drunken laughter. "What other do you think, when I plan to use them in here?"

"You think you're ever so smart, don't you?"

"Ah, but I am a wise man."

"Are you, now?"

"Wiser than you've ever met." Traveler leaned over to snatch a hasty, greedy kiss. Lightning nipped at Traveler's lower lip when he drew back, then glittered with pleasure as Traveler dove back in for another kiss that nigh split both their lips.

"Teach me a lesson, then," Lightning breathed in challenge.

Traveler climbed upon the bed. *Lords bless us both if we've remembered or once thought of putting any clothes on today. Would that it could be so all days.* The words Lightning spoke made him tingle. Hadn't he relished the thought of fucking some manners into the youth? Now he begged for them.

Well and well, a lesson he would *get*.

"By all that we both hold holy, be as a wax doll in my hands," Traveler said as he took Lightning's wrist and fastened the end of one leather strap around the slim bones. He forgot, for the moment, how his phrasing half-invoked yet more of the magics he'd already been over-generous with. "Lie you still, lover, and let me bind you to set you free."

It was the sort of thing he'd have expected Lightning to balk at, but nay, Lightning glowed with interest and let himself be manipulated.

Sorcery, Traveler would realize later, and curse himself for being more than thrice a fool.

191

At the moment, he had passed mere giddiness and was well on his way into thoughtless abandon. He kissed Lightning between the fastening of each strap to wrist and then ankle-bones, teasing his cock with a flickering tongue. As the bed was made in a round shape, he had nothing to fasten the far ends of the ties with, but no matter. A small whisper to the winds, and they came from North, South, East and West to tug the bindings tight, pulling Lightning's arms and legs wide apart.

Lightning's breathing quickened. Equally drunk, as Traveler would comprehend later, on magics and sex, he voiced no questions about *how* he could be held fast. "You have me at your mercy, then?"

"I do." Traveler took up his peacock feather and began running it across Lightning's chest. He pushed the bulbous head of the dildo, broad enough to torment any man and delight him beyond measure, against Lightning's hole. The stone had been kept oiled and was smooth enough besides that it slipped right in, nice as you please -- but just the head. Just enough to tease. The youth's nipples perked into hard knots and a line of herald seed trailed away from his cock to pool on his belly. He groaned, pulling against the straps.

But ah, he couldn't touch himself, could he? Couldn't touch Traveler, either.

Traveler felt, but dismissed, the surges of power within him as he whispered: "Now, my Gypsy love, we play..."

Chapter Eleven

A light spring rain graced the faire grounds, city and island the day after. Lightning had lost count of the times he and Traveler had made love. Every muscle he could name ached, yet in a good way. He stretched slowly to enjoy their protest. After all, he'd earned these strains for sure and certain...and loved every minute.

Their morning's fucking had eased into an afternoon languor, filled with soft kisses, light caresses, and the occasional lewd joke. Lightning had heard most of them before, but now he truly got the points and oh, how Traveler did laugh and tease him when he blushed.

Sipping lazily at a warm mug of spiced wine, Lightning felt like a prince. Traveler's island held such riches! It almost made him think about the caravan, and how what he'd once thought fine paled in comparison...

He put the mug down with a hard *thunk* on the sill of the window where he stood, looking out at the lawn, the rocks and the sea. "Bedamned with that," he muttered. "I shame my family line, thinking such things."

"Eh?" Traveler asked from where he had

Faire Grounds

lain himself down and stretched out on a few of the pillows from the other room. "Did you say something, Thorn?"

Lightning twitched. A few days before, he'd have had no trouble telling Traveler in no uncertain terms what weighed on his mind -- he'd have flashed and thundered like his namesake and what an argument there would have been.

Now, his lips closed instead of spilling out accustomed angry words.

The enchantments of Younger and Peddler must run deep, he thought. *It's the bond that softens my tongue. I would protest...but, somehow, I'm not feeling that I can.*

Nor do I know why I should care.

What was I thinking of?

Ah, never-mind.

Lightning picked up his mug and took a thoughtful sip, clove and cinnamon dancing over his tongue. Good, this was good...still... "I ought to go," he said abruptly. "I really ought to. There's work needs do, yet I linger here."

"What harm in taking a day or so of rest? You've just been wed, after all; no one would expect you not to enjoy yourself for a while and a while." Traveler had, in his cupboard, found some fruit he claimed grew in his gardens. They were like nothing Lightning had seen before -- small green ovals that popped between one's teeth with a rush of sweet juice. You had to be careful of the jaw-cracking seeds, though.

Grapes, Traveler had called them. Lightning wondered vaguely what such a delicacy would fetch on the road, and puzzled once again as to why Traveler did not go abroad at least part of the year to turn a profit on his treasures.

I suppose I hesitate to leave because once I do, I'll have to face a myriad of choices for the future.

While I bide here in this place at this time, I can put off thinking about things I would not that I had to ponder.

"Stay," Traveler encouraged. "Pretty Lightning of the long black hair, my Gypsy love. Stay. We can play again soon. Would you like to be the rider this time, and me the stallion?" He cupped his naked balls with a leer. "I'd even let you put a bridle on."

Lightning's mouth tipped up with good humor. Get to know him, and Traveler was a merry man indeed. Truth to tell, the thought of feeling the man's thick cock inside once more made him prickle eagerly.

But there, there, they had time, and really, if they *didn't* take a rest, they might easily fuck themselves to death. *The body needs food and sleep and exercise,* he remembered Horsetail teaching him. *Neglect one and you may as well cast aside the rest. All three are necessary for good health -- to do whatever you will with, eh, Silverfish?*

The realization of the double meaning in Horsetail's aside made Lightning wince, not without good cheer. They'd been so in love, his fathers. Enchantments or no bringing them together, they'd been true mates-of-the-heart for so long as he'd known them, and through

Faire Grounds

all the years before.

A grape bounced off Lightning's head. "Hoy! Stop your games. Those are too precious to be wasted."

"Think you? Well, perhaps. I wanted to get your attention; you'd drifted so far away. Where did you go?"

Lightning lifted one shoulder. "Old memories. My fathers."

"You've spoken of them before. You were raised by two men, aye?"

"Raised by two fathers. Love bound them so tight together that when Slipstream, who was the older by some years and long sick with the illnesses of age, passed over to his rest, Horsetail -- still more or less young and strong besides -- followed him a handful of days later."

"And you were twelve."

"As you say." Lightning inclined his head. "They'd taught me well, though, and I managed fine as -- peacock feathers -- once I was alone."

"And what did they teach you?"

"Trading. Driving the caravan." Lightning reached out to touch the window. "Enchantments. Love, though if you'll recall, I had my problems with the notion."

"Aye. Love." Traveler fell silent for a moment. Lightning heard him bite into another grape and spit the seed out. "What, then do you now think love...ah, never mind."

"What?"

"No, never you mind. We'll talk of other things."

Lightning marveled at himself. Not so very long ago, he'd have hounded Traveler until the man gave up his secrets. Now he found himself content to take direction. "What would you speak about?"

"Mmm. What strikes your fancy?"

"A good question." Lightning glanced around himself. Now he had time to study them, he saw the intricate carvings on every window-frame and sill and around the doors, plus paintings and sketches everywhere one could be tacked. They all showed the fine hand of a Master. "Have you always been an artist?"

Traveler chuckled. "No, not always."

"Tell about how you learned, if you please." Lightning turned from the window to sit down, legs crossed beneath him, mug of ale carefully balanced in his hand. "I want to hear the story."

"Stories, tcha. Children are the ones who love stories."

"I think I have proved I am no child," Lightning replied archly, though with none of the acid tang which would once have been second nature. "Humor me."

Traveler stretched his arms above his head -- mmm, such long, toughly muscled arms, Lightning could almost forget what he was about and lose himself in thought of being wrapped in those arms -- oh. He blinked back to himself.

"It's a long story," Traveler said thoughtfully, scratching at his belly, bare as it had been since they'd begun their wedding leave. "Give me a moment to organize this in

Faire Grounds

my head..."

(Lightning did not know then, but would know after, that Traveler took this time to alter the tale from its true bones and shape them in a different light.)

"You can read and write, aye?"

"Aye. A good clear hand."

"Not so mine. I can write, yes, but my script is appalling and the good Gypsy who taught me my letters despaired of anyone ever being able to *read* them. Others tried, but gave me up as useless with my hands." He paused. "All but one."

Lightning leaned forward, falling into the tale as Gypsies did, his attention keenly focused as Traveler went on in dreamsome sort of way.

"We met, upon the road, a man called Grigori -- by the Grounders. With us, he was Hearthstone. He it was who changed my life forever, or at least this part of it. It was he who saw that while I despised writing rows of letters, art was a bloom ever-growing inside me. It was he who saw how my boy's hands were forever busy plaiting handfuls of reeds into designs or drawing pictures in the road dirt with a stick.

"He saw this as a good thing. Others -- as I am sure you know -- were wary of drawings and images. Bad luck, so they said, and forbidden by the Lords of the Road."

Lightning nodded. Horsetail and Slipstream hadn't held with those particular taboos -- they loved beautiful things -- but he knew a few of the older clans who felt thus.

"Before Hearthstone found me, my art brought me naught but ill luck. After a few beatings, I learned to satisfy my cravings on the sly. I would borrow cooking knives from the woman -- and oh, they were dull, ugly things -- the knives, not the women, although they were fairly soured by life themselves. I foraged for sticks thicker than my thumb but not thicker than the circle of forefinger to thumb, and when all else were asleep, *I* stayed wakeful and indulged in art, carving those sticks into anything I could think of, from work-a-day to utter fancy.

"I always threw them away before morning's light, or burned them in the remains of the camp-fire. One old Auntie would have done the burning for me, and boxed my ears until they burned as well, all the while filling my head with lectures of how evil I must be."

Lightning made a noise of sympathy. Horsetail wouldn't have struck a woman, no, never in his life, but his father would have had a few sharp words to say about such cruelty.

He felt fortunate in growing up as he had, and listened all the sharper to Traveler's tale.

"Bah, I wander from the point. I was speaking of Grigori -- Hearthstone, I mean. He came upon me one bright morning when I had nodded off over my work the night before. Eve after eve of little to no sleep takes its toll, after all. Auntie had woken early and found me with knife and stick, and Lords, but her temper blazed fierce. She'd warned me and warned me, but I wouldn't listen."

Traveler paused. "It was in her mind to

sever my forefingers with the same knife I had used, so I could not do this again."

Lightning sat bolt upright, horrified. "Surely someone would have stopped her?"

"Someone did; Hearthstone. I was old enough to fight back, and too foolish to know I was only digging myself a deeper hole, and so I wrestled with Auntie over both the stick and the knife. We must have made the racket of a dozen fighting cats, for Hearthstone came out of his wagon still rubbing sleep from his eyes and inquired, ever so gently, as to why we were raising such a fuss."

So that is where he learned the trick, Lightning thought, remembering his first meeting with Traveler.

"Auntie had respect for Hearthstone. She had to; he was one of our clan who had some wealth and her elder besides, though he seemed far younger to me. She made bold in accusing me, thinking Hearthstone, like the rest of the clan, would take up her side. But instead of saying 'yes, yes, go on, Auntie', turned and asked me: 'And what do you say, boy?'

"I showed him my latest carving and blurted out every word of the whole sorry tale. Auntie grew whiter and tighter-lipped with every word I spoke, and I knew she would have punished me sorely, but I could not have stopped myself if I had wanted to -- which I did *not*. Hearthstone's eyes did not judge, and he patiently listened to me for so long as I had breath to go on."

"And his judgment?" Lightning pressed, impatient. "I see you still have your fingers, so..."

Traveler plucked another grape from its bunch and lobbed it at Lightning. "Who tells this, you or I? When I had done speaking, Hearthstone held out his hand for the stick, which I gave him. And although he had heard me out without condemning my soul, I feared he'd break the wood over his knee and tell me to mind my elders at the very least.

"Instead, he turned the carving over and over in his hands -- short, stubby hands, good enough for wielding axe and short-sword, or horse's reins -- and brought it near the fire only for more light to see the artwork by.

"My heart thumped so hard in my chest it hurt me as I waited for him to speak. He frowned at me over the stick for so long and long a time, it seemed to go on forever.

"Finally, he spoke, not to me, but to Auntie. And to her, he said, 'Never, never scold this lad again, and may the Lords of the Road have mercy on you for such cruelty to a child.'"

"He was more forward-thinking, then?" Lightning inquired.

"Eh, he'd traveled further than they and understood the world a good deal better. To any rate, from that moment on I rode in Hearthstone's wagon, and was left to draw and carve to my heart's content. Whenever we crossed paths with another artist, he handed over coins so I might learn another thing or two. I stayed with him 'till I was some years older, and we parted ways as good friends.

"And there! There's my story told."

Traveler grinned at Lightning. "So sober. Did I disturb you?"

"No, not really...well, somewhat."

"How so?"

"I cannot help but wonder at how close to you came to disaster -- to being *mutilated* -- and I am amazed at your good fortune." Lightning looked about himself, troubled further still. He would *not* ask why Traveler had gone to ground, not yet, but... "Good fortune has been yours ever since, aye? Whatever goals you set, you accomplish. Whatsoever you desire, it becomes yours."

"Not everything," Traveler denied, rising to brace himself on one arm. "And not always easily, in truth. I think I know what you think now. You think whatever strange luck I have tickled at your family's enchantments and turned them to its own advantage. But no, Lightning, no. Bristly thing, I would have avoided you if *you* had not forced the issue."

"I only wonder..."

"Wonder no longer." Traveler made his way to Lightning and laid a chaste kiss on Lightning's lips. "We are tied, you and I, beyond any luck or enchantment. Trust me on this."

It would be so easy to believe.
For a little while, I will not question.

Lightning closed his eyes as Traveler kissed him again, more hungrily this time, and laid his hands on Lightning's skin. He touched back, fingers roving with increasing happiness over hard muscle, tweaking at nipples and laying down light scratches. His cock swelled again, eager to dance once more, and when he put his hand in Traveler's lap he knew Traveler felt the same.

Then, Traveler flinched. No, not flinched -- jerked back and away, as if he'd been struck by a bolt from Lightning's namesake. Lightning would have sworn he saw a wisp of smoke, and for true he smelt burning hair and flesh.

He sprang into a crouch, every nerve on edge. "What's this?" He reached for his ankle dagger before remembering he was bare of clothes as well as weapons. Beyond the stench of burning, he picked up a hint of cold stone and something he couldn't name, something that raised all his prickly quills. "Is it a spirit?"

"No." Traveler shook his head, looking dazed. "Nay, Lightning. There is a -- a fault in this house -- this sometimes happens when the rain falls -- bide here, and I'll go see to fixing that what's gone amiss."

Lightning shook his head. "I go with you."

"No!" Traveler planted his hand in Lightning's chest and shoved him hard enough to fall back and land on his arse. The man's face was a fearful thing to see as Lightning stared up in shock. "I must do this alone. Stay here. You're not hurt. Stay, and wait for me."

And without another word, he hurried away into the room with the pillows, slamming the door behind him.

Lightning sat, stunned as if arrow-struck, and stared after him.

Lords of the Road, what...?

Faire Grounds

* * *

Traveler threw back the screen covering his long-abandoned working-room and made straight for a mirror he had covered in a length of shroud-cloth. Behind it, the glass glowed red-hot.

"Oh, the hells you will," he breathed, reaching out for a certain powder he had made sure to keep in easy reach on the table. It would be old, but should still suffice. He flung a handful of the floury stuff at his mirror. "Away! There is no one here you need to seek."

"I should think this is exactly where to look," a sibilant voice mocked, the crystals of Traveler's potion deflected harmlessly away. "Did you think you could run forever, Janos?"

"Traveler. My name is Traveler."

"*Janos*. Son of the King. Runaway Heir. I *know you*."

"Name yourself, then. Who are you to seek this man -- who I am not?"

"Do you think me stupid? Names hold power, and I know you retain your wizard-skill. You've certainly flung enough magic-stuff about in the past day and day before that even the daftest hedge-witch could trace you."

"Who -- are -- you?" Traveler gritted out. "I'll know who you are, if not what you're called."

"One who knew you well, yes, very well, when you were still a Prince. One who you made a promise to, then broke your word. I told you I would not be played for a fool,

Janos. I have learned a few things of my own, and now I have found you, I *will* see you dance to my tune again."

Rosalind.

Janos -- Traveler -- Janos -- put aside the question of 'how'. He could easily figure the 'why'. "What do you want of me?"

"I will speak of something else, first, which you may find of interest."

"Do not toy with me," Traveler warned.

"I? Toy? With you?" Rosalind laughed, the sound no less musical or cold for coming through the mirror. "Your brother, Andrei, lies dying of a rotting pox he got from a two-copper whore. A string of women who claim to have borne his babes besiege the castle, demanding money and that their sons be recognized. They beg in vain, for Andrei has all but drained the treasury, idiotic wastrel that he is."

"Things fare ill in the land where I was raised. Why should I care? They turned their backs on me, and I on them."

"Ah, but you are a *good* man, aren't you, Janos?" Rosalind crooned. "I will tell you more. The people starve here. Babies grow thin and die because their mothers lack enough milk to fill their bellies. Dogs run like wolves through the streets, devouring whatever is weak enough to stumble and fall. And though the houses are crumbling, everyone hides inside for fear of curses Andrei laid upon them in one rage or another." She cooed. "You would not leave these people in such a state, would you? Not you, Janos. You cared. Even when you walked away, you cared. I can feel your pain at my words. They cut like silver sewing scissors, *snip-snap*."

Traveler's throat burned. Such suffering -- was it true? "Why do you involve yourself?" he forced out the demand. "The woman I once knew would not have cared one clipped copper half-bit for people in pain."

"And I still do not. But you do, and thus I have you. Come back to your kingdom, Janos, and give me what you once promised. Andrei will be overthrown, the coffers will fill again, and the land will return to health."

"You have so much power?"

"Janos, I am and ever have been far more of a force to be reckoned with than you dreamed. I order you now to come back to me."

Lightning. Lords of the Road, Lightning.

"And what will you do with me, once you have me?"

"Whatsoever I please," Rosalind said silkily. "You will come. If you protest another word, then I will find my way to whispering in your young Gypsy's ear. He shall know the truth about who you are, where you have come from, how you have tricked and fooled him since you were bound, and how you came to him in secret invisibility."

Traveler stood stock-still, mouth open.

"I know all of these things, and more. Come back to the palace, Janos. Come tonight, or I will do as I have promised. Lawbreaker. Forsaker. Liar. Come to me, Janos, come, and I will take pity."

"Lightning --"

"Will be safe and sound, and I daresay even happy, while you are away. I have asked, but you have not answered. Yes or no, Janos?"

The words stuck like sand on his tongue, but Janos -- Traveler -- Janos spat them out at last. "I will come."

"At once."

"Yes. At once."

Rosalind giggled, a sound fit to fill a man's heart with terror. "Then I'll be seeing you by nightfall, won't I? You can travel swift as the wind, Janos, I know. Fly to me, and all will be well. Until we meet again...my Prince."

The mirror went dark and silent. Janos stared at the malevolent thing for a moment. Then, with a roar of frustrated rage, flew forward and shattered it with both his fists.

* * *

"I must go."

Lightning looked up in surprise. Luck had padded along and appropriated his lap, and he'd been biding his time more or less content that Traveler would soon return and they would pick up where last they had left off.

Instead, Traveler was clothed in garments elegant as any from Slipstream's trunk, and had a broadsword he buckled to his belt besides. "Traveler?" Lightning asked in wonder. "What goes here?"

"None of your -- I cannot tell you, Lightning, my thorn. Would that I could." Traveler crouched, seized Lightning by the

Faire Grounds

back of his skull, and dragged him close for a desperate kiss that tasted of bitterness and bleak despair instead of joy. "I must go."

"Go where?" Lightning demanded, making to stand up. Luck growled and dug his claws into bare flesh, and thus he was prevented. "Traveler?"

"I'll return as soon as I may." A shadow shifted in Traveler's eyes. "Wait for me, Lightning. Wait until I return or word comes that I never will."

"Traveler!"

"I cannot explain. Do not ask! But wait for me, Lightning, wait for me." He looked as if he wanted to kiss Lightning again yet did not trust himself to let go should he come too close. "Take my boat back to the faire grounds. Take all my love with you."

"But where are you going?"

"Where I must. Forgive me for what you see me do now."

Lightning's protest was ready in his throat, but died as he saw Traveler stride forward... and disappear into nothingness.

Sorcerer!

And...

Gone.

Gone for how long? A day -- or forever?

Luck purred on Lightning's lap, kneading his leg. Lightning held the massive black cat close, but refused to cry against its fur, neither for fear nor in anger.

Not to shed a tear at all.

* * *

Somewhere In the faire grounds. Night:
"Ah, there you are. Well-met, my friend."

"Bollocks. You're not my friend, nor am I any of yours. And whatever you call yourself, you've no right to come inside my family's tent at this time of night. You nearly woke them as well as myself, and then what would I have done, hey? Hey?"

"Such rudeness."

"Pfah! If you'd been wanting manners, you'd have sought out someone else, or been well-advised to. What d'you think I am, your lap dog?"

"No. I *know* you are. Now listen well, little cur: he leaves tonight. I am sure his intentions are to stay only a fleeting time, as little as possible, and then he flies back here to his Gypsy lover. Mate. What-will-you; the terminology wearies me."

"As if their unions were legal, any road."

"Well put. As I said, though, he is gone, and that means he comes to *me*. I will keep him here for far longer than he expects. And the longer he bides, the more his lover will want to have word from him -- a shameful waste of parchment, in my opinion. You know what to do."

"Hah. So. Well, I'll not back down now. I gave my word."

"And do you prize your word so dearly as do the Gypsies?"

"More so than the one you're hounding. A liar threescore over, he is."

"And it does not bother you that what you are swearing to do is against the laws?"

"What do laws have to do with Gypsies? That which protects them isn't for keeping their hides safe. I'll do this and sleep well at night. And speaking of which, now we're met and agreed, d'you mind? I've an early morning."

"Peasant. Count yourself lucky that I have a use for you, and that you amuse me. Otherwise, I would turn you to glass and strike you with a hammer so you fell about in broken slivers."

"Ah, bah. I have no care for threats."

"Truly, you do amuse me. Very well. Our treaty is sealed. I will make good on what I offered you: your life, and the other small boon."

"Ever so kind, you are."

"Peace. Return to your bed, wake to your work, and do as we agreed."

"Aye."

"*There's* a good pup, so there is..."

"Pfah!"

Hasty steps hurried away from the place of meeting.

In the darkness, the voice which had spoken from nowhere laughed, a cold and silvery pealing of bells...

Chapter Twelve

The journey to Rosalind took an eternity and bare seconds all at the once; such was the nature of traveling with magic's aid. Traveler -- he would not call himself Janos, not at anyone's command -- had beckoned the winds again, this time asking for their speed of travel, begged birds for the loan of their light bones, and for good measure asked hares for their speed. All agreed, for they liked Traveler, and missed the days when he'd often spoken to them as friends.

And so he sped to his old home swift as an arrow from the bow, albeit with a heart brim-full of dread and his teeth gritted in loathing.

Traveler knew the castle well enough to cease his voyage in the center of the throne room, where his father and father's father before him once sat to listen to the people and dispense justice, where great lords and ladies had, upon a time, gathered to make or renew treaties, then celebrate over fine foods while they drank well-aged wine.

His father's kingdom had been a peaceful one where crops grew thick and lush, all animals brought forth plenty of young for meat, wool and milk, women never miscarried and all were plump with good luck, deeply contented with their lives and with full trust in their ruler.

It had been a good land full of great fortune.

Which was why, when Traveler came to a stop in the throne room, his first glance around made him choke with dismay.

Hand-woven tapestries worth fortunes had been stripped from the walls, only their rusted hooks proving they had ever been there. The marble floor, once polished daily to a gleam, was covered with filthy, matted straw. Through the strands, Traveler could see how black the marble had been begrimed before someone had given up the job and laid down a peasant's flooring. The solid wood benches on which villagers had sat to watch or wait for their cases to be pled were gone -- but splinters and an axe left to spoil in the corner told Traveler of their fate.

Outside the windows, left carelessly open -- where they were not broken, costly colored glass ruined beyond repair -- Traveler could hear a woman keening the death-song of a newborn. Carrion birds swooped in and out, diving for rotting foodstuffs among the straw. A parliament of rooks had taken up residence in one corner, cawing at him in mockery.

Though he dreaded to, Traveler looked up at the throne. "Andrei," he said without thought, heart sinking. His brother sat barely propped-up against one arm of the carven chair. His hair did not seem to have been washed in weeks, nor his clothes, once fine but now frayed and torn and covered in food spills.

Traveler could see the marks of pox on Andrei's face in angry red boils and sores that covered the most of his lips.

Andrei looked up and cackled, the wheeze of a man far, far older than his years. "Have you come back for me to kill you at last?" He fumbled where a sword should have been, then grunted as he reached for an ankle-knife. That holster was empty, too. "Damn. Sold them on," he grumbled. "Someone! I know you're out there. Bring me a blade!"

A figure shimmered into being behind Andrei, a woman of surpassing beauty, or so Traveler suspected men who liked her kind would describe her. The finery she wore, a full dress gown embroidered with pink posies and decorated in pearls, seemed an obscene contrast against the ruin of the throne room.

She laughed, silvery-clear.

"Rosalind," Traveler spat in disgust.

She coolly raised one neatly shaped eyebrow. "So. You did come. I had my doubts. For someone with your distasteful interest in the male sex, I wondered if your young Lightning would have been too much of a temptation to leave behind." She smiled, and it was like unto the glimmer of ice. "But you came to me. You always come."

Traveler heard a note in Rosalind's voice he liked little. She sounded as if, now he'd come, she owned him and crooned over him as if he were no more than an amusing new pet.

"What's happened to bring all this about?" he asked, refusing to rise to her unspoken challenge. "Such ruin. How did it come to

Faire Grounds

pass?"

Rosalind clicked her tongue, even such a common gesture dainty when the noise came from between her lips, painted a deep rosy pink. "Grammar, Janos, if you please. You sound common as the Gypsies you traveled with. Not a King's son at all."

Traveler deliberately deepened his accustomed accent to match the roughest he'd ever heard on the road. "Be you not a-pleased? I be a Gypsy by right, for I've spent years on years with mine own adopted Kin. I'll speak as I like, so I will."

"I could freeze the tongue inside your mouth. Appalling manners. But it pleases me to dispense mercy." Rosalind patted Andrei's crusty shoulder. "Yes, yes, settle down, there's a good fellow."

"Kill 'im," Andrei muttered. "Kill 'im. Wine. Bring me wine. An' if we have none, bring me ale. An' if there's none left, go and fetch a barrel from the village. They're hiding some away, the sots, I'm sure."

"In a bit you will have all you want to drink," Rosalind soothed. "I have other matters to attend to first." She looked back at Traveler. "So, you have seen the changes wrought during Andrei's rule. He emptied out the stores of gold to amuse both friends and sycophants, then sold everything once precious to further pay for his entertainments. When he had nothing left of value, I came."

"To gloat over the wreckage?" Traveler asked bitterly.

"Oh, no, no. I waited until then to come

because Andrei no longer had any power over me. Poor man, he'd already begun to suffer from this pox." She petted Andrei again. "His sword, and I do not speak of the long-bartered blade of metal, had already rotted away with sores and his muscles wasted. He could not hurt me." She flashed another smile. "So I came in and made myself at home, as you see."

Traveler found himself unwilling to dally with further words. "Enough of this. What do you want *me* to do about this, Rosalind?"

She shrugged delicately. "I'll leave you to think on these questions: what do you want to do? And another: what can you do? One more: what are you willing to do?" Her slender hands clapped together. "Now, go and think. I've prepared a room especially for you."

A chill wind, not friendly as were the ones Traveler had ridden on, buffeted him from head to foot. He found himself hurtling through the air, unable to bid them cease, down a rotting stairwell and into a dark room made of cold, dripping stone, more foul rushes laid upon the floor. A skeleton hung on one wall, shreds of leathery flesh yet clinging to its hide. Its mouth hung open as if in a final death-scream.

There, the winds dropped Traveler flat on his arse. As he struggled to get up, he saw Rosalind appear at the open door. She dimpled at him. "Do you like your accommodations?"

Traveler would have roared curses at her, but found himself too choked with rage to make a sound.

"Get used to them, deserter -- of road, of

throne. Think upon the riddles I have posed, and wait. I will be back in a bit to see if you have discovered any solutions. Oh, and Janos -- do not think you will escape. I have secured these walls against any magic, black or white." She tittered. "Enjoy your stay."

The door slammed, revealing heavy wards painted in gold leaf on its back. Traveler stared at them, shaking his head in despair, then sat heavily down in the rotten straw.

Lightning, was all he could. *Ah, Lords of the Road, watch over my Lightning now!*

* * *

Although he ill-knew how, Lightning had taken Traveler's boat and rowed it ashore, then tied the craft into place with good hard knots. The knots themselves were well done, but he took no pleasure in his handiwork.

He stalked up the banks toward where the Gypsy's portion of the faire grounds lay with his lips tightened in a thin line.

As he might have prophesied, those out and about greeted him with sunny good cheer and abandon. "Welladay, the new husband!" one bellowed in greeting.

"Where's your handfasted? So soon away from him?"

"Belike he's coming soon. Eh? Coming?" The speaker roared with amusement at his own jest.

Two Gypsies, alike as peas in a pod, danced up to his side. "How is Traveler? We didn't meet at the ceremony, you and us, but we know him of old and wish you naught but joy."

"And how do you like being wed, young Lightning?"

"Does good luck follow you?"

"Is your husband as kind a man to you as he seems?"

They were crowding in too close. Such was the Gypsy way, for they touched as casually as they breathed, and as many as spoke, more clapped him on the back with grunts of approval.

Lightning felt as if he could not breathe.

"Enough!" he burst out. "Away from me, away! Leave me alone!"

Startled, his kinsmen drew back. Their cries died into a shocked silence.

"Well," a well-padded tinker's wife huffed after a moment of dead quiet, planting hammy fists on her hips. "There's gratitude for you, eh?"

"Hush," her husband ordered. He turned his back on Lightning. "If he wants to be left alone, then we'll leave him be, the lot of us. So say you all?"

The Gypsies maintained their grim silence as they turned to different courses and melted away. Lightning knew he'd offended them deeply, and that they would not speak to him again unless he begged their pardon.

His temper burned too hotly to consider such a thing yet. Let them harry him with silence; he cared not. He had business to attend to, and a caravan to go over, and later horses he'd want to check in on where they grazed in the small pasture the faire grounds had allotted

Faire Grounds

to Gypsy beasts.

Lightning's precious goods seemed intact when he examined them, and so he hoisted himself into the caravan next, glaring at the immaculate interior. What right had this home to look so welcoming and serene when...Traveler's island...when Traveler...

One thing out of place, or rather in a new place, sprang out at him. A sheet of parchment folded twice over, laid in the center of his pallet where he could not miss the thing.

A letter? Who would be after sending him such?

Lightning whisked the parchment up and folded it open. The script was abominable, but after squinting a bit he got the hang of the misshapen letters and read:

Lightning,

You've gone to your home. Good. It shows you have a bit of sense. I had my doubts, after all, with the way you've behaved. Stay where you are. I command you not return to my island. That is my *home, after all, and none of yours.*

I told you I would not be gone long. I have changed my mind. I have reached the place I sought, and find it most pleasant. I'll tarry here so long as it suits me. Do not look for me to return soon. Perhaps not before the end of the faire. We will see.

Do not attempt to answer this communication. I will not tell you where I am, nor how to get here. I wish to be alone, away from your clinging grip and childish ways; I have grown tired of your limping wit and your prickling moods.

Perhaps I will not return at all. If I do not come back before faire's end, you may consider our 'union', such as it is, dissolved.

I sign this with no love.

-- 'Traveler', as you have known me.

Lightning lowered the paper. His eyes stung, but as he had done the night before, he refused to shed a single tear or betray his hurt in the lines of his face. Easily as he had been wont to do in the past, he drew shutters down over any hint of what he might be feeling.

Wooden, he climbed out of his wagon and busied himself with kindling a cooking-fire.

But although it was in his mind to burn the letter, in the end -- he did not.

* * *

"Janos?" Rosalind teased. "How are you enjoying your stay thus far? Are the quarters to your liking?"

Traveler was not at all sure how long she had left him down in the dungeon with only a skeleton for company. There were no windows, and nothing to mark the time.

Instead of answering, he glared up at her, so perfect and pristine, not setting one of her silken-slippered feet on the grimy steps.

"You must be hungry." Rosalind snapped her fingers daintily and held out her hands for a half-loaf of bread to appear in the palms. She tossed the food down to Traveler -- far out of his grasp, which he knew she had done on purpose -- into the stinking straw.

Though his stomach rumbled with hunger, Traveler refused to give Rosalind the satisfaction of seeing him crawl like a dog after scraps. He stayed put, and demanded, "What do you hope to accomplish by keeping me down here? Is it for your own amusement? Revenge for when I put you aside?"

"A bit of this, a bit of that." Rosalind tilted her head, painted lips curved up in amusement. "Although I will admit it *is* most satisfying to see you brought so low. But I have not come to tittle-tattle. Tell me: have you thought about my questions?"

"I have." Traveler got to his feet with some difficulty; the air in his prison felt full of the ague that sapped a man's strength. Probably was fouled so a-purpose. It would be like Rosalind to play such a petty game. "My heart tells me I would do anything to repair the damage Andrei has wrought, but my mind tells me you have a card up your sleeve, a nasty trick you've in mind to play, and the price you will ask of me is likely more than I can pay."

"La, la, you can pay, if you please. But will you pay willingly? I have learned the art of truth-tell, and I will know if you lie in hopes of an escape."

"Bah! Either speak plainly as to what you want, or go away. I find his company more enjoyable." Traveler pointed to the skeleton. "He may be a quiet sort, but I'd rather the peace of the dead than your prattling."

Rosalind's good humor flashed into irritation. "Time away from your proper place has lowered you, Janos. You dare speak so to a lady?"

Traveler snorted. "Lady? I see no ladies. All I spy is a half-mad she-witch."

Oh, there was a touch, a sting. Rosalind darkened with the flush of anger. "If you were not...if I had a choice...oh! Or do you hope to aggravate me to the point where I might lose control?"

Damn; cunning as ever she was.

Rosalind composed herself. "I will let you know the price I demand. The sooner you are willing, the sooner I will set you free."

"Free from this dungeon alone, or from the castle altogether?"

"What do you think?" Rosalind tittered, not covering her mouth as courtesy dictated. "But come now, here's what I propose. Take me back, Janos -- or rather, agree to stand at my side and confess how you wronged my reputation. Take me to wife."

Fury nigh-blinded Traveler. He fought against the rage and to clear his head. "I am already handfast to another."

"So I have learned. Gypsy marriages are not legal. Bastards, the lot of them, in all senses of the word. You are quite free to wed me, I assure you."

Traveler spat on the rushes. "I would sooner die."

"Then perhaps you will. I care not." Rosalind shrugged, delicate as a flower. "Stay here and rot with your fellow man a while longer. In the meantime, I will seat myself upon the throne as your proxy."

"That seat is occupied by Andrei."

Faire Grounds

"Not any longer." Rosalind's teeth looked sharp in her smile. "Oh, did I forget to tell you? Your brother is dead. The kingdom is without a leader. Think on that, too, if you will. And for now, farewell."

She closed the door.

Traveler fumbled his way toward where the loaf had landed, unable to see a thing in the dungeon's pitch darkness. He found the bread with his fingers, feeling at once how it was the coarsest of loaves, stale as a rock, something even a beggar might be disinclined to set his teeth in.

He hurled the loaf against his dungeon's door with a bellow of frustrated fury.

It made him feel no better.

Bedamned to you, Rosalind. I'll ne'er marry her, the bitch. But Lightning...she does know of Lightning...my Thorn, though I cannot protect you, may you please be safe, and wait for me...

* * *

"What the hells? What do you think you're doing?" Lightning scrambled out of his caravan, landing indignantly on both feet.

The two faire Guards picking and sorting through his packets of tea ignored him.

"That's my stock, my wares to sell, mine by right!"

"Not no longer," one grunted with malicious pleasure. "The faire's called for a tax on Gypsy wares. Half of what you have to sell -- all of you -- is due to them in charge for allowing you to stay."

"Half?" Lightning's head reeled. "I don't believe you."

"Believe me or believe me not, it's all one so far as I'm concerned." The Guard kept picking up bags of tea and stuffing them in a rough-woven basket he carried. "The rest of you, I'll be along shortly. Make ready your wares, and don't be after hiding a thing! I'll search your wagons to be sure you're holding nothing back, I and my Guard-brothers will."

"He's brought bad luck with him," Lightning heard a Gypsy grumble. At the man's words, a host of angry eyes landed on Lightning, scorching marks on his skin. "And what'll happen next, I ask you?"

"Shut your foul-breath'd mouths!" the Guard barked. "What comes next will be exactly what pleases us and our rulers. You can't fight us. If you try, then you're out of here and all your stock stays behind."

"Bad luck, bad luck, bad luck," the Gypsies murmured.

Lightning pinched his lips shut and turned away with shoulders stiff.

* * *

Once again, there was no telling how long Rosalind had chosen to leave Traveler alone in the dark. He had spent time waking and sleeping, waking and sleeping, finally growing hungry enough to crave the bread she'd tossed down -- though he refused to bend and eat it.

He tried to use his magic, calling upon

every cantrip and trick he knew to no avail. Rosalind had spoken true. The dungeon's wards rendered him helpless as a babe.

Save for one thing.

When he tried a particular spell to regain his strength, the skeleton began screaming, the shrieks of raw despair and the terror of certain death.

Traveler was only a man. He fell to his knees and pressed his hands to his ears, trying to block out the blood-chilling noise.

But in the end, he screamed too.

* * *

Lightning,
I am most displeased with you. How dared you sail across to my island? I have told you once to stay put, and with disgust I command you again: keep out. Set foot on my property again and I will see you cast into the ocean.

I can do this, as I am sure you suspect. Foolish Lightning. Did it never occur to you I might have more than ordinary magics? That I might be a wizard? So naive. So childish. A good fuck, as the case proved, but as I ponder matters of greater import, I begin to regard our time together as nothing but a lark.

And you believed every word of love I spoke, silly Gypsy. It amuses me to think of how easily you fell.

I will write again when it pleases me.
Until then, mind my warning.
-- Traveler (or perhaps you should call me by my true name: Janos)

* * *

"Have you changed your mind?" Rosalind demanded from the top of the dungeon stairs. She had changed into another elegant gown, delicate blue as the sky on a fine day. Gold flowers decorated her glossy, artfully arranged hair.

But for all her neat presentation, Traveler could see the temper boiling beneath the venomously ladylike façade. Despite the ague settling hard in his bones and the hunger raging in his belly, this amused him.

He managed to raise his head far enough to bark, "No!"

Rosalind's mask slipped long enough for her to snarl at him. "Then lie down there and rot!"

As the door slammed, Traveler lay back on the dirty straw and thought: *were it not for Lightning-my-love, who I promised my return, I would gladly die down here before I gave her what she wanted...Lightning...do not despair of me, dearest Thorn...*

I will find my way back to your side.

* * *

"Lightning?" A light, nervous rat-a-tat of a knock sounded on the side of his caravan. "Lightning, are you to home?"

Nell's voice, full of concern that stung Lightning's pride as would the bite of an adder.

He made no reply.

"He has closed the wagon, Nell, and taken his goods inside as well." Lightning heard

Meilin murmur. "Clearly he desires no company. It may be just as well to leave him in peace."

"Leave him?" Nell protested. "We're his friends, we are. It'd be a poor friend who walked away when he's in need -- aye, I know you lot can hear me, Gypsies one and all. *I* remain faithful." She knocked again. "Lightning, do let us in. Or if you will not, then come out to us."

Lightning lay flat on his cot. He'd had his trousers open, stroking at his cock, at first straining after memories of Traveler's touch, insistently believing they had worked him with love, true love, and then stubbornly when his prick refused to rise.

"Nell, I advise we leave him to himself."

"No," Lightning snapped abruptly. He laced up his trews and kneed to the back of the wagon, where he opened the sealed curtains. "Come in, if you will. I'm not welcome outside, and bedamned if I go where they disdain me."

"Oh, Lightning," Nell murmured, hand going to her lips. "Lightning, you look terrible. Have you eaten or slept at all these past few days?"

He had not, but refused to admit any such thing. "I am well."

"May we?" Nell asked, already clambering up. "Lightning, we've been that worried over you, ever since the rumors came you'd returned alone after your handfasting."

"So, folk are talking." Lightning's heart felt turned to stone.

"The people always have and always will

prattle about anything striking them as good fun, or with malicious intent." Meilin pulled his hands out of his sleeves. "May I, too, come in to join you?"

Lightning welcomed neither, his prickles up at their intrusion, but Nell was already inside and reaching for him, so where was the harm in granting Meilin's request? "Come." He dodged away from Nell. "But do not touch me."

"As you wish." Meilin climbed in with a much greater grace, and settled himself easily in a crouch on the caravan's floor. He regarded Lightning with his customary patient silence, content to wait all day or leave without any further words spoken.

"Here." Nell fumbled in a drawstring bag hanging off the belt on her dust-brown tunic. "I knew you wouldn't be eating, so I would -- no one thinks to take a meal when they're bereft -- and here, I've brought you this, as a gift."

The offer was an insult, but Nell was, in the end, a Grounder. Perhaps she didn't know, aye. And to refuse would be bad manners. Lightning might have been shunned by the clans, but he still held to their customs. He took the clay bottle she offered him and gave a stiff nod of thanks.

"Go on and drink," Nell urged. "'Tis nutritious stuff, it is, healthful as a full meal. It'll do you no end of good."

Meilin chuckled. "I would not drink such a thing if my life depended on the consumption, but do as you will, Lightning."

Faire Grounds

Dubious, Lightning uncorked the bottle and sniffed at its contents. He could not but help pulling a face. "Pfaugh. What's in this?"

"Clabbered milk, for one. That's what you smell. The yolks of chicken eggs. Ground wheat. And fruit, see? There's berries ground in for flavor. I paid extra for those." Nell sounded proud, all-unknowing of the debt she incurred. "Go on and have a drink. They're all the rage through the rest of the faire."

Lightning glanced at Meilin. Meilin simply smiled and shrugged.

He took a sip. The first impulse was to spit the slimy, sour-milk concoction out, but swallowed in determination. He got a faint taste of ripe berries as the drink slipped down his throat.

Lords of the Road help him if he'd take another draught, though.

"The things folk do when such is in fashion, eh?" Meilin said with a twinkle.

"What? You don't like my gift?" Nell looked deep-hurt. "Drink more, Lightning. The taste grows on you, and you've lost weight, I can tell."

"I'll save this." *Aye, until it's wholly rotten.* Lightning corked the bottle and put it aside. "I'm not hungered." And in that, he did not lie. "So. Folk are chewing me over as they might a tasty morsel. I'll have none of your pity, I warn, so if that's all you've come to offer you might as well be out again."

Nell's kindly face creased further with concern. "Lightning, we only wish you well."

"Then leave me alone." Lightning turned

his back. "I thank you for your gift, and for the visit, but I would you were on your way now."

"But, Lightning --"

"Hush, Nell." Lightning heard Meilin's robes rustle as he rose. "He desires peace, and if we are his friends in truth, we must grant him his request."

"Lightning, will you let me kiss you for luck?" Nell pleaded.

Lightning refused to turn around.

"Nell. We go, and now. Lightning, should you decide you do want a taste of company, Nell or I will gladly return. Now come, Nell."

Lightning kept his face forward as his two visitors climbed out of the caravan.

He kept his shutters down even when he heard Nell complain, as they walked away, "I would have asked him where Traveler has gone, and why. Shame on the man, to leave his new-mated husband so!"

"Such matters are none of our concern. Leave well enough alone, Nell."

Lightning stared forward, the stone in his heart spreading through his limbs.

It will be good to be stone. Stones have no hearts of their own which can break, no, nor do they have any tears a-begging to be shed.

I shall be as a stone. Aye. I shall.

* * *

"Well? And what do you say now?" Rosalind smiled benevolently at Traveler, who had long since collapsed, unable to stand.

Lightning, I love you, Traveler thought, then swallowed. "How fares the kingdom?"

"Passing poor," Rosalind replied with an air of indifference. "There have been riots, I hear. Folk frightened by the lack of a king take to thieving what they can from merchants, though they're poor as poor alike. Women fight like starveling mongrels over bits of rotten food from midden-piles." The intensity of her gaze deepened. "But you can change all this, Janos. Only agree to what I ask, and I will restore this land to what it had once been."

"You swear?" Traveler croaked, his throat so dry that speech was painful. "Will you make the magic unbreakable?"

"By my soul, I swear. Let the magic I use bear witness against me: what will be done cannot be undone. May I be stripped of all my power and rank and beauty if I forsake this oath." Her face grew hungry. "Do you agree, then? Will you make me Queen?"

"The guiding star you've sailed by all these years. Aye. I will make you Queen."

Rosalind laughed, coldly beautiful and triumphant a sound. "Then out of the pit with you!"

Traveler glared.

"Oh, poor man. Are you too weak to climb on your own? Here, I'll lend you a bit of strength. There! Now you can walk. Come to stand by my side, and we'll go out together."

Rosalind's magic stank of overripe hothouse blooms and sickly perfume, but Traveler gritted his teeth and accepted her offer, gathering his legs beneath him. He shook a bit, but he walked upright, step-by-step, until he stood at her side.

She drew away with a moue of distaste. "Ay me, what a stench. And what a sorry sight you make!"

What did you expect after days down there? Traveler wanted to snap -- but did not.

"This is easy enough to fix." Rosalind laid the tip of one finger on Traveler's nose, as if he were a child, then stood back again as her magic did its work. Grime disappeared from his skin, oil from his hair, stains and rents from his clothing, and ague from his bones. When all was done, she regarded him with a look of smarmy pride. "There's an improvement. You look quite the Prince again. Now. Follow me."

Lightning...

Traveler fell in obedient step behind the Lady. "Where do we go?"

"To the terrace overlooking your -- our -- courtyard. I've laid a compulsion on the people, and they will already be gathering with the knowledge that we will speak. They have hope, Janos, hope that what they come to hear shall cure their ills." Rosalind cut Traveler a sly look. "And you will not deny them, will you?"

"I'll keep my word, and I'll see to it the folk are taken care of."

"Good enough. Lavender's blue, dilly-dilly, and rosemary's green, dilly-dally, and when you are king, dilly-dilly, then I shall be Queen..." Rosalind trailed ahead, singing with malicious merriment.

Traveler made no response. He simply kept

Faire Grounds

walking, head down.

When they arrived on the terrace, things were as Rosalind had predicted. The once-fine villagers, now thin as sticks and dressed in rags, had packed so tightly into the courtyard Traveler wondered how they managed to breathe. To a man and woman, all faces were tilted up to gaze at the terrace.

They even cheered when first Rosalind, then Traveler, stepped out.

Rosalind bathed in the adulation for a moment, then lifted her hand for silence. "Good fortune to you, my people. And yes, you are my people now, for I am to be your Queen. Good fortune to you."

Traveler felt the tingle of magic and knew Rosalind had already begun the spell of reparation.

"May health return. No more babies shall die, nor their mothers. No more fights nor riots. May your crops grow thick as thieves and your livestock fatten round as barrels."

The pallor of dull despair began to lift from the people. They stood up straighter, with the light of startled delight in their eyes.

Traveler watched, rejoicing as best he could. And waited.

"This land will return to what it once was, and so shall it ever be. There!" Rosalind swung around to look at Traveler. "Lift your head, Janos. I have made good on my bargain. Now, you keep your word. Declare me Queen."

"Very well," Traveler said, his voice low and low. "You are Queen."

He raised his head to look at her, all the

magic he had been denied blazing from him. "And Queen you shall be!"

The power of his sorcery hit Rosalind as would a fist between the breasts, knocking her flat on her rump. She tried to fight free of her billowing skirts and aimed what was no doubt meant a punishing blast against Traveler. "Behave yourself!" she hissed.

"Aye, I will, though not as you intend." Traveler faced the people with all the might of the Prince-Heir he had once been. "Behold Rosalind, your Queen. She will be a good ruler, fair and just. Her words will come true, just like magic, and not a bit of what she has promised will fail." He grinned back at outraged Rosalind. "So she has sworn. And she will keep you safe when I have left, as I will immediately."

Rosalind snarled at him, her beauty marred by ugly rage. "Your word. You promised."

"I said you would be Queen, and Queen you are." Traveler allowed himself a small smile. "Never once did I say I would be your husband. And you have bound yourself, Rosalind. You have made the people healthy and whole, and you shall rule over them with a gentle hand."

"I'll crush them like dogs."

"And lose your beauty, among other things?" Traveler shook his head. "No. I know you, Rosalind. You would die before suffering homeliness. And here's my magic: you will meet a man who masters you, who enchants you, wed him and bear him a daughter with the gentlest and wisest of hearts. When you are gone she will reign better than any before, and

Faire Grounds

her daughter and that one's daughter after her. Think of this, Rosalind -- you found a line of Queens."

Traveler called upon the winds again, and found them clement, eager as puppies to do as he bid, and strong as wolves to carry him on their backs. "Rule wisely and well, lest you bring about your own doom," he said in final warning before he let the breezes catch him. "All hail the Queen!"

And he was gone.

Speeding his way back to Lightning.

Laughing all the way.

Not aware of how Rosalind, rising from her tumble of skirts, understood what she had gotten herself into -- but, with what power she still had, taking her revenge...

* * *

Lightning,
This will be my last letter to you. You have afforded me great amusement, and now, we'll have one final joke.
I will tell you the truth about what I am, and who I am, and savor the thought of how you were so easily fooled...although it was not hard, given how you are a fool in truth...

Lightning laid down the letter. "I am stone," he said quietly to himself. "I am stone."

But he was yet a Gypsy.

He made his way unerringly to Slipstream's trunk, and rustled within until he found, on the very bottom, that which he sought.

Drawing the object out, Lightning regarded its sharp blades with neither favor nor disfavor.

Scissors, sharp enough to cut canvas, glistening as if new-made.

"I am stone," Lightning said, and caught hold of his braid. He brought the scissors close and began to cut off his long locks. Watching them fall, he felt nothing.

"I am stone," Lightning repeated as he sheared his hair close to the skull. "Stone. Stone. Stone."

And he did not rage.

And he did not cry.

He did not cry at all.

Chapter Thirteen

"Ease, winds. Cease your gales. Let me down -- gently -- if it please you." Traveler spoke with due reverence for the forces of nature.

They appreciated good manners. Something else he'd forgotten. Magic didn't care to be tossed about all willy-nilly, nor flung about like wheat for doves. Magic was an entity all unto itself, and it liked its due respect, for sure and certain.

Traveler had lost sight of what he'd been taught by those older and wiser, but he'd not forget again.

The winds eased Traveler to a rest on his feet, light and easy as if he'd been a feather they carried merrily along. Tendrils of breezes tugged at his ankles, though, so he'd not forget the forces were yet there.

Traveler bowed at the waist as had once been drilled into him as a Prince, though with the light-hearted spirit of a Gypsy. "My thanks, fair winds. You've served me well. Now go, if you will, and blow where it pleases you."

Warm air blew in Traveler's face as if the wind kissed him like a favored son, then whirled away, catching up leaves to toss them about in good-natured play. He watched them go.

Perhaps they'd come again later to put on a show for Lightning if he asked nice enough. It was a good thought.

Now, though, he had landed a league or two from the faire grounds. Although he would have been there in a hurry, he judged it would be better to stroll in by his own means. Where there were Guards there would be Lords, and where there were Lords there were likely to be Mages. He'd been foolish in his hasty departure -- Lords of the Road, not even a novice might have missed him. He felt fairly sure they couldn't have identified him, but he'd show more caution in his return.

Best not to rouse their curiosity, or possibly their ire, by tempting fate twice over.

Whistling to himself, thinking happily on a reunion with Lightning, his dear Thorn -- who would, no doubt, prickle something fierce after being left so abruptly and for so long, but Traveler could ease him down, he could. He knew his Lightning fair well. A kiss, perhaps three, and maybe yet more if they could find a private spot...mercy, he knew *he* wouldn't be able to wait on a sail out to his island, and Lightning would surely have come back to tend his wares.

He felt full-confident as he fell into the loose, easy strides that quickly ate up distance, the Gypsy-walk he'd not used in years but neither forgotten. The knack came back with ease, and soon he'd covered a distance that pleased him with his speed.

Faire Grounds

A walking-stick, though, that would have been nice. He didn't need one, being neither infirm nor lame, but all walking Gypsies carried such and it would have made him feel more the part.

Well, why not?

Traveler detoured from the road to the faire into a copse of sturdy maple trees on the verge. There'd be a fallen branch or two about, to be sure, and one of those would do excellently fine for a Gypsy-stick...

Whinny

"Eh?" Traveler stood upright so quick he near bashed his head on a heavy limb. "Who goes?" Odd. He'd not seen nor heard any riders before or behind him...

Whinny, he heard again, with a note of insistence. No one else answered his call. Curious, Traveler pushed through the trees and emerged into a meadow rich with thick green grass. Close at hand stood a fine black gelding, elegant and well-groomed as the pick of a prince's stable. The horse snorted and shook its head at Traveler, then pawed the ground and turned about so his side faced Traveler.

Entertained, Traveler stroked the horse's sides. "Lords of the Road, be this your doing?" he asked, though he expected no answer, and in truth, got none. He checked the gelding for brands of ownership and even magical ties, but found nary a thing. For all he could tell, the horse had simply come from -- somewhere -- and decided it wanted Traveler to have a ride.

"There's a bit of unexpected luck. I'm sorry, fellow; I've neither apples nor carrots nor sugar for you. But when you've carried me where I'm bound, I'll find you a fine treat, and there's my word."

The horse snorted.

"All right, all right." Despite the lack of stirrup or pommel, Traveler swung himself easily onto the horse's bare back and squeezed with his thighs. "I'm guessing you'll know the way. Off we go, then. And while we travel, I'll tell you about my light-of-love. Lightning is his name, and aye, he'll like you too, for he's an eye that appreciates beauty..."

"Janos? Janos, is that you? Traveler?"

The crackling voice surprised Traveler more than the gelding's appearance. Had he reins, he'd have pulled his mount to a stop. "Nikka?" he asked, disbelieving his ears. "What the hells? How are you contacting me?"

"Through the horse, you nincompoop," Nikka scolded. "Though you've lost your necklace charm, this gift of the Lords you swear by has permitted me to use him to make contact."

Traveler glanced curiously at his steed. "Does he speak the truth? Is that no lie, but Nikka himself I hear?"

The horse whinnied again, conveying as much disdain for human foolishness as the cat Luck at his finest. "Easy, there." Traveler petted its arching black neck, the hair softer than any he'd felt on a beast before. Near soft as Lightning's tresses unbound. "Nikka, you and I must needs have some words. Why did you not tell me things had gotten so bad in the

Kingdom?"

"I would have. I *tried*." Nikka sounded impatient. "Rosalind's foul magics stopped up my throat time and time again. She toyed with me, Traveler. The words I spoke were not the words you heard. Else, you'd have heard my cries for help long since."

"So," Traveler mused as the horse stepped lightly on. "She lied to me. She's been around for a goodly time, and not just since Andrei sickened."

"You expected any other but lies from her? Were you still a child, I'd take you over my knee, I would. Aye, she's been lurking about since you left, in one guise or another. Sympathizing with the King over your loss, spilling poison in his ears as to how it was all for the best, then attaching herself to Andrei when the King passed over. Where she learned magics, I don't know. Mayhap she made a bargain with dark forces."

"Sounds likely. Rosalind never did care what means she used to accomplish the end she craved. But tell me, how are things? Do the enchantments hold fast?"

Nikka chortled. "You should see them! Straggly fields are full to bursting, and the reapers are hard at work. Folk who were stick-thin have plumped out once more, and there's apology after apology flying in the air as they make amends. Rosalind sits on the terrace yet, and oh, she's ill-pleased at the trick you played, but she knows she's bound fast by her own words."

"She'll rule well, or lose all she has." The

horse shook his mane. "Easy, there," he soothed. "I've no grudge against you, Nikka. Go and enjoy the renewal of the Kingdom. Make merry, and when I next call, let me hear nothing but good news."

"I've no doubt you will. Fare well, Gypsy who refused to be King."

"Fare you just as well, you old rascal." Traveler felt the contact *pop* free. His horse neighed with great indignation. "Hush, now. If you're to be a wizard's steed, you must get used to such things."

The beast snorted again. "You're touchy as my Lightning, so you are," Traveler remarked in admiration. "Dark as you are, I'll call you Thundercloud. Now forward, my bonny fellow. I've been too long gone, and glad will I be to return home once more."

Thundercloud seemed to understand. He began to gallop, running for the fun of running, carrying Traveler lickety-split toward his destination. Traveler whooped and hung on with all his might, gleefully speeding toward his beloved.

And as he rode, he bellowed out a Gypsy traveling-song, reveling in his new-found and well-reinforced freedom. No more death-threats hanging over his head, no more ties to being royalty. All he wanted would be waiting for him in the Gypsy encampment, and soon he'd be there, so he would.

Ah, he could hardly wait!

* * *

Faire Grounds

The rollicking delight Traveler felt dimmed considerably when he faced the gates. The Guards posted there were twice as sour as the ones who had stood watch when he first came in, and Traveler saw piggy greed in their eyes as they examined Thundercloud for any sign that he'd been stolen.

"No Road-trash rides such a fine horse," one spat to his fellow, who nodded with an unashamed lust to claim Thundercloud for their own.

Thundercloud was a good lad, though. When he'd tired of the Guards' poking and prodding, he turned into a bucking, spinning dervish, baring his teeth and taking nips at the pair, some of which hit home. The Guards cursed and backed away while Traveler, hiding his mirth, pretended to wrestle Thundercloud under control.

One Guard wiped his mouth free of blood where the horse had grazed his chin with one flying hoof. He spat again. "Touched by evil, that one is. Let him go with the Gypsy. Aye, let the whole sorry lot scorch themselves on his fire."

"Am I free to go, then?" Traveler inquired mildly.

"Bah! On your way." The Guards opened their gates. One tried to kick Thundercloud as he trotted past, proud head held high -- and Thundercloud kicked back, his aim wicked as well as true.

There was one Grounder who might find breeding hard in the future.

Placid as if he hadn't noticed a thing,

Traveler rode on.

And what he saw inside the faire grounds disturbed him, further dampening his good spirits. Merchants and buyers and idle visitors were out in force, aye, but they hissed and drew away from Traveler as he passed. The ugliness in their expressions was like unto Rosalind's in the height of her fury. Most glared, many made the sign against evil, some hissed insults, and a few even threw sticks and stones.

Thundercloud neatly dodged all the missiles and Traveler closed his ears to the Grounders' cruel words.

All the same, he worried. They'd been none too kind to the Gypsies before, but now they made no effort to conceal a definite hatred. What would he find in the encampment?

Traveler didn't know, but would not turn back, oh, no. He'd a mate to find, and if possible he'd call on magics to protect the lot of his Road-kin along with Lightning. The Grounders didn't know what they were up against now, they didn't.

He'd see how bad things were, first.

And he'd have a kiss from sweet Lightning, so he would.

Without urging, Thundercloud picked up his pace and made his way unerringly along the paths leading to where Gypsies had been thrust aside. "Good fellow," Traveler murmured. "Good fellow. Let's hurry up and have a look at my -- our -- kin, and see how they fare."

He had an ugly feeling about this.

* * *

Faire Grounds

All but the faintest flicker of good cheer died as Traveler entered the Gypsies' part of the faire Grounds. A somber mood hung thick and heavy over the usually jubilant folk, most of whom hunched over their wares with a suspicious, watchful air. They examined him most narrowly as he came through on a fine horse.

"Grounder?" he heard one man mutter.

"Nay. He's dark as any Gypsy."

"His horse is too fine not to have been taken in the tax, or by the Guards, pox riddle them all."

"No, he's a Gypsy for true. Methinks I recall his face..."

"Is it --?"

"Fie; cannot be."

"No, no, she's right. This is Traveler."

"Traveler. Aye, Traveler."

Their recognition of him spread like ripples in a pool, but as many and many eyes fastened upon him and his horse, they remained suspicious and ill-pleased.

Lords of the Road, what had happened here?

Two handsome young men approached and would have crossed his path. Thundercloud came to a stop, sniffing at their dusty clothes. "Lightlaugh?" Traveler queried in surprise. "Fairlaugh?"

They turned sullen glances on him. "So, you've come back."

"Better that you had not."

Murmuring soothing words to Thundercloud, Traveler slipped off the horse's back. "You sound as if you're upset with me, you do. Tell me, what have I done? An' if you'll speak to me, tell me why the Gypsy camp has changed so."

"Guards and taxes, taking half of all our goods. And I'm Lightlaugh no longer; I'm Ill Wind."

"Is this true, Fairlaugh?"

"Nay, no longer Fairlaugh. Call me Bitter Wind. My brother speaks true, and there's more besides. The Grounders have dammed up our water, so we've no place to bathe or wash clothes and precious little to drink. The horse meadow has been sown with salt, so the grass for grazing dies. Now leave off. We're on rounds this morning."

"Rounds?"

"Aye. We're seeing who has enough food left, and who's lacking. Though what we're to do with those that hunger, I know not. Conjure edibles from thin air?" Bitter Wind's laugh was bitter indeed.

"I can -- I can help --"

"We'll not be indebted. Come, Ill Wind. We waste our time here."

Traveler blinked in surprise as the pair, who he'd shared many a merry and lusty hour with, passed him by. They treated him as if he weren't of the Kin, either road or Gypsy.

The bad feeling he'd developed made his stomach sour. "Is Lightning well?" he called after the twins.

They made no response.

"Go and see for yourself," a voice raspy from thirst said from down below. "He's the cause of all our bad luck, or so they say."

Traveler looked down at a woman he vaguely recognized, then realized he knew her better as sparkling and frolicsome, dressed in gay colors, rather than robed in a dull brown sack with her hair scraped back into a tight knot. A poor Grounder's outfit, not a Gypsy's garb at all. "Lightning has brought you bad luck?"

The woman sniffed and returned to stirring her pot of thin-looking broth over a meager camp-fire.

He'd get no more out of her, he wouldn't.

Traveler walked on, worried half out of his wits, and ever more determined to rejoin his Lightning. Bad luck? What bad luck could his Thorn have brought?

When Lightning's caravan came into sight, Traveler winced. Its bright colors and fanciful decorations, gleaming as if new and freshly-washed, seemed to mock the drab gloom settled on the rest of the camp. None but a fool could mistake such a thing as other than magic. No wonder the Gypsies had taken a dislike.

Lightning himself was nowhere to be seen, nor any of his stock. The caravan had been closed up tight, canvas flaps at front and back fastened nigh impenetrable. Traveler saw no signs of any recent blaze in the tossed-about stones of what had once been his fire-pit.

Worry gnawed at him with ever-sharpening teeth. "Lightning?" he called as he drew near. He knocked on the side of the wagon. Lords of the Road, what if his Thorn lay injured or dead inside? Gypsy curses, and no doubt some had been uttered against him, if they did truly hate him so, could be powerful things.

"Lightning, it's Traveler. I've come home again and I would make amends for leaving in such a rush."

Silence was his only reply for a bit.

Then, the flaps at the back of the wagon parted. Lightning stood in the opening with arms crossed over his chest and legs planted far apart. He glared at Traveler with all his prickles out.

And his hair...sweet mercy, his hair! Traveler choked down a noise of dismay. Every inch of that glorious length was gone, naught but stubble taking its place.

"Lightning," he did whisper in dismay. "Lightning, my love. If I can ask anyone what's come about, it must be you. Tell me what's happened to these folk, this place, yourself?"

Lightning's glare faded into utter flatness. His beautiful face turned harsh and cold, as if carved from stone.

"Lightning?"

"Come inside," his handfasted mate said with no emotion. "I'm not welcoming your presence, but I'll not speak to you where there are others to hear."

"Not welcoming...?"

"Come inside if you're coming, or stay out. I care not."

Traveler patted Thundercloud's flank. "Stay put," he ordered quietly. Thundercloud had, it seemed, grown solemn as the rest and moved not an inch. Even he seemed dimmed by the despair that choked the encampment.

To be on the safe side, Traveler drew a quick magical circle in the dusty ground around his horse's body. Where had the lush, thick grass gone?

Then, he climbed up into Lightning's caravan, despite limbs gone heavy with worry.

Once inside, the light was all but too dim to see by. Though he suspected Lightning had been cloistered here for -- how long? possibly days -- the wagon smelled fresh as a daisy. "Lightning? Would you offer the kindness of a candle or a lantern?"

"For a fair trade, I might. Cast a spell to be sure and certain no one hears us."

"Lightning?"

"I'm less the fool that I was before," his Thorn snapped. "I know you can do this. Shroud the caravan in silence, and I'll strike a light."

Who had told him such? Traveler vowed to find out. In the meantime, though, he'd do as he'd been asked. He laid his hands on the caravan floor, and felt magic billow out, spreading willingly through from wheels to canvas roof.

"It's done. Will you trade and trade alike?"

"For the sake of Gypsy honor, aye."

Traveler heard Lightning scrape at a flint. The spark was near bright enough to hurt his eyes after they'd grown accustomed to the gloom, but eased as Lightning fixed a spark to the wick of a lantern. He placed it on the floor before his pallet, and sat with the grace of a marble statue come to life.

He displayed all of such a statue's emotion as he waved Traveler down. "Sit, if you will, or stand if you choose."

"I'll sit." Traveler eased himself down, deliberately closer than he suspected Lightning would like in his present mood, but too stubborn to do otherwise. "So you know I can work greater magics than most. What else do you know?"

"By and by I'll tell you." Lightning touched his shorn scalp. "What do you think of this? Tell me honest and true."

Traveler answered honestly. "I grieve at the sight. If I remember aright, and I believe I do, your family only shears their hair when they mourn. Why do you grieve so?" He reached out, wanting to touch, but Lightning jerked away. "Talk with me, if you will. Please. I need to understand this division between us."

Lightning made a noise that could have been worth a thousand words, or mean nothing whatsoever. "Here." He reached back onto his pallet and came up with a stick of Traveler's own soft lead plus a scrap of parchment. "If you would have us talk, then I'll have you do something first."

"If it lies in my power, I'll do my best to please." Anything to break through Lightning's stony shell. "What would you ask of me?"

"Write."

"Write?"

"Aye." Lightning thrust lead-stick and paper at him. "It matters naught what you scribble about, but put something down. I know you said once your handwriting was a horror, but I'd see for myself now."

Traveler peered at his mate, but found no clues in his immobile face. Wary, he took the writing materials offered and moved back a little so he could brace the parchment against the caravan floor.

Words deserted him for a moment, then came in a flood:

Lightning, beloved,

It's a deep regret I had to leave you so, with hardly a word of warning and nary an explanation. Know, however, I missed you with all my heart while we were parted, and that I have dreamed of the day when I might take you in my arms again, kiss your sweet lips, unbind your hair -- your hair! -- and smooth it down. To unwrap you of your clothes as one might strip the wrappings of a gift, for a great gift you are, and go down on my knees, aye, my knees, to rouse and taste your cock once more. I --

"Enough." Lightning thrust out his hand. "Give me the paper."

Traveler obeyed without question. Perhaps script would serve where speech had not as yet. If Lightning could read his abominable scrawl, that was.

Lightning held the paper to the light of his lantern and frowned at the script Traveler had writ down. Oddly, he neither squinted nor tilted the paper to puzzle out Traveler's handwriting.

As he read, Traveler waited, hoping against hope Lightning would let down his prickles and soften into the pliant, lusty lover he had left behind.

Too much to dream of, he realized, puzzling further as Lightning scowled fiercely. "Be this your idea of a joke?"

"Joke?" Traveler blinked. "Why would I jest over such a thing? I have set down what I feel. Every word here is truth."

"Truth. So you say."

"So I swear."

"Your word. Bah. I know what your word is worth." Lightning thrust his hand beneath the sleeping pallet and drew out a thin stack of parchment sheets. "The script matches, and I've not only learned to read the way you make your letters. Here." He pushed the papers at Traveler. "I think you'll be remembering these."

"What?" Baffled, Traveler glanced over what Lightning had given him. He gave a start of surprise as he recognized his own dreadful writing...and his heart sank in despair as he read the contents.

Letters. Letters addressed to Lightning, all of them calling him "fool" or making mock of the youth. Cruel and cutting barbs bristled at him from the pages. He read through one or two, then could bear to read no more. He laid them aside, feeling befouled. "Where did you get such things?"

"They appeared in my caravan, on my pallet. Seven in all, one for each day you were gone. I've learned much from what you sent me, Traveler. Or, as I should call you, Prince Janos." Darkness flickered over Lightning's stone-face. "Grounder. Liar. Deserter. They say it's me who's brought bad luck to the Gypsies, but if I have then it's from my contact with you. Fool you called me and fool I was to believe your falsehoods."

Traveler had gone numb. *Rosalind must have done this,* he thought, seeming far away inside his head. *Bitch! She's not only put the spoil to my love, but she's betrayed me into the bargain.*

He shook his head. "I never wrote such things, beloved."

"Don't call me that."

"Never a word of them," Traveler insisted. "I -- I -- it is truth that I was born a Prince and Grounder, and was given the name of Janos. But when I was close on your age, I left that life behind. Gypsies adopted me, taught me art, taught me magic. I am not who I once was, I swear."

"And your promises mean so much. You lied about the mossy rocks to heat your water, you lied about the grapes and such treats, you lied about the wards upon your home." Traveler saw the glimmer of darkness again, deeper black this time around. "You lied by omission by never telling me *you* were the one to slip into my caravan and take your pleasure with my body, all invisible."

This, he could not deny. "Forgive me," Traveler whispered, looking down. "I have no excuses save that I wanted you so badly when I snuck in, and I only meant to please you thereafter."

"You lied again by omission in not telling me you were a wizard."

"Only for your own safety." Traveler moved closer, trying to touch Lightning's crossed leg, but Lightning moved away flicker-quick. "If you had known about my past and why I had learned the magics I used to keep me safe from those who would have me return to the life I left behind...forgive me, Lightning. I did not give you worthy credit. I should have told the truth from the start; I see this now. Forgive me? We can begin again."

Lightning examined him flatly. "No," he said. "I do not forgive you, and we will have no new start. I know not what game Younger and Peddler's enchantments were playing, but I'm done. I love you no more."

Traveler felt something inside his heart begin to squeeze and crumble. "I have no hope?"

"None."

He spread his hands. "Then what will become of us? I love you still, and ever will until the day I die. Truth, Lightning, only truth."

Did he see a flash of yearning? If he did, it was quickly hidden. "Your love comes at too high a price. I am the one bewronged, and so it is my choice as to what will happen now. Even you should know this is the Gypsy way."

Traveler winced at Lightning's scorn.

"A handfasting need not last, if one or both of the bound wish it dissolved."

"You would do such a thing? The enchantments --"

"They are satisfied for another generation."

"But what will you do?"

Faire Grounds

"Travel alone. Gather more tea to sell. In time, adopt a Gypsy son and raise him in the hopes that he will have better luck than I."

"Lightning, please, no."

"I will do as I see fit. I --"

Knock! Knock! Knock!

"Lightning?" A light-hearted woman's voice. "Lightning, I know you're to home. I've come to visit, myself and Meilin as well. Oh-ho, the flap's already open. We'll pop inside for a bit of a visit, shall we?"

Traveler glanced at Lightning. Ah, his façade had slipped a bit to show anger. "Nell, keep out," he barked.

Nell ignored him, lifting skirts of rich blue to step into the caravan. She chuckled as she brushed them free of travel-dust. "I've another of those drinks for you. La, la, how the other folk love them. Truth, I've developed a taste myself. This one is flavored with blueberries. You should like it well enough -- *oh!*" She had finally looked up, and on instinct Traveler turned about to face her.

Their eyes met, and in hers Traveler read both anger --and -- fear?

"What's he doing here?" Nell snarled, her good cheer evaporating fast as fog. "How in the hells? I thought -- I was told --"

The pieces fell into place.

Traveler needed no magic to move quickly enough -- slow-moving, clumsy Grounder -- to grasp the hem of Nell's far-too-rich skirt and give a hard tug, setting her off-balance and bringing her down hard. "Give this message to your mistress, if she'll speak to you again," he hissed. "Her trick has failed, her vassal caught, and the game is over."

"Traveler?" Lightning stirred on his pallet. "What do you mean by this? What do you accuse Nell of?"

"These!" Traveler grabbed the so-damning letters and waved them in Nell's face. "Did you write them yourself, or did Rosalind deliver them by magical means? How did you slip them into the caravan?"

"Traveler?" Lightning sounded confused. "Nell?"

Traveler turned back to plead with Lightning. "There was a Lady who would have been Queen of the kingdom where I was reared; she it was who summoned me back, and kept me prisoner, aye, until I outwitted her schemes. I'm certain as I can be she sent these notes. Smell them. Go on, get a good whiff."

Lightning took the papers. His stony expression had gone completely as he raised the letters to his nose. "Roses," he said slowly. "I smell roses, and some sort of sickly perfume. I never before..."

"She knows she's been found out. Roses from Rosalind, don't you see? Now she's been discovered, the power fades and the truth comes to light. Believe me, Lightning, please. The Lady who captured me played a cruel jest to drive a wedge between us. She sent the missives to you, not I. Believe me."

Traveler's Gypsy youth looked uncertain as a boy. "I...I know not...Nell?" He looked pleadingly at the woman. "Nell, *is* this part of your doing?"

Nell laughed, and it was not the sound of a sane woman. "What do you think, little fool? Did you actually believe a Grounder would befriend Gypsy scum? My Lady Rosalind dictated the letters, aye, and guided my hand to mimic Traveler's script, but I meant every barb and sting as if I'd come up with them myself."

"Why?" Lightning sounded heartbroken.

Nell cackled again, ever more cruel and cutting. "My Lady has promised me many things, and promised to make good. But you should never have doubted my honor for a second. The drinks --"

"Potions," Traveler corrected harshly.

"Drinks, potions, what-have-you." Nell huffed like an indignant horse. "You never drank them, did you, you little ingrate?"

"They were foul to me." Lightning inched forward. "*Why?*"

"I've told you what I've told you, and you'll get nothing more." Nell kicked at Traveler, taking him by surprise. "Let me go!"

"The hells I will." Traveler sought to find another grasp of her skinny legs. "I'll see you harried to the end of your days for what you've done."

"No," Lightning said, quiet as a mouse. "Leave off, Traveler. Do as she asks. Let her go."

Traveler released Nell in surprise. The wench wasted no time in hurling herself out of the caravan and running away fast as she could scurry, never once looking back. He itched to bring her down with magic, but stayed his hand, for Lightning had requested this of him. "You would have her go unpunished for what she's done?" he had to ask, however, astonished.

Lightning looked aside and did not answer.

"If you will permit me to speak?" Traveler flinched at the new voice until he realized Meilin stood yet outside, hands folded in his sleeves. He bore a look of mixed regret and compassion. "I may have some light to shed. I knew her best, after all."

Lightning refused to look at the man-from-over-the-mountains. Traveler made the decision for both of them. "Speak. And ware what you say. If you confess to being any part of this, I'll punish you no less harshly."

Meilin nodded. "These are fair terms. I will not come inside. I trust Lightning will be able to hear me; he can hear a twig snap in the forest from a mile away, or so he has said. I knew nothing of Nell's treachery -- not in specifics. Whoever she served cloaked her origins well enough to fool almost everyone, but ah, that woman did not count on *me*." He gave what would have passed for a ferocious grin in any other man. "I could smell magics on Nell when they first touched her. Rotten roses and perfume. So I kept an eye on her, careful as I might be. I did what little I could and rendered her potions harmless, if foul. They were not poison so far as I could ascertain, but I trusted them not."

"Why not act? You knew she was up to something, and you didn't stop her?"

Meilin lowered his head. "She would not listen. I believe now she was bespelled to turn a deaf ear to anyone who would distract her from her mission. And what else could I do? I have not sufficient magic to ward the caravan...not when I am away from the road...and so long as I am here, I am no match for Nell in physical strength."

Traveler frowned at Meilin's speech, but put the man's words aside to think on later.

Meilin continued. "Short of taking her life -- and I am sworn against murder -- or calling down the guards -- who would not have come, but laughed at her needling a Gypsy -- I could do nothing but watch, wait, and pray to the Road Lords for intervention."

"How did she get the letters into the wagon?"

"We may never know." Meilin raised his shoulders. "Perhaps more of her Lady's spells covered Nell's tracks. Mayhap she laid a charm on an animal to sneak her venom in. Animal..." He narrowed his eyes. "Lightning, what of your cat? Patpaw?"

Traveler turned to see Lightning's surprise. "I've hardly seen her since I came back to the caravan. Patpaw?" He made clucking and cooing noises. "Patpaw, are you in here?"

Ah, there's a bit of the softness he hides so well. "Allow me," Traveler said gently, prodding the small tabby out of her hiding place with a nudge of magic. "Here she is. She smells of roses, Lightning."

"Meow," Patpaw voiced, looking far more miserable than any cat Traveler had ever seen. She hunched into a small lump and meowed pitifully.

"I do not think she had a choice," Meilin

offered. "I have some skill with animals, and from what I can see she was forced to do Nell's bidding."

"Ahh, Patpaw." Lightning petted the tabby's dulled fur. "Rest easy, sweetling. I've no grudge against you." He looked at Traveler, and oddly. "I have learned much to change my set opinions on things in these past few minutes."

Traveler felt a surge of hope.

"I will leave you two alone together, then. Only, a word of advice? Forgiveness is far sweeter than hatred, and vengeance coats both heart and tongue with bitter ash." Meilin regarded them with sudden cunning. "I venture to say your fathers Slipstream and Horsetail would second my words. Now, I go."

"We'll see you again soon?" Lightning inquired.

"No, I think not." Meilin tilted his head to face the west. "I depart these faire grounds, which are not so fair at all, as soon as I may fill my pack and walk away. I'll take to the road, wherever it leads me. I may go so far as to return to my home over the mountains. Do not worry for me. I will be safe, and I will think of you often."

"Meilin, I will *miss* you."

"I have plenty of years left in me, and so do you. We will meet again." Meilin bowed at the waist. "Fare you well, and blessings on you both."

Traveler and Lightning watched the small man in black slip away, silent as a ghost, not even disturbing the dust at his feet.

Traveler whistled lowly. "I would pay a fortune to know his whole story."

"He'd never tell."

"Think you?"

"I know, for I asked once upon a time, and he fell to telling parables that made no sense, teasing me all the while."

"But there *is* a story behind him. There must be."

"Aye."

Traveler hesitated, unsure of himself despite the candle of hope burning within. "And now that he is gone, what will become of us? Do you still wish for us to part ways, my Thorn -- may I still call you mine?"

"Traveler?"

Traveler turned to Lightning. The youth's face was a study, but his harsh lines had softened, and he looked like a lad again, not a statue nor a sour elder.

He waited a moment, then spoke. "Traveler, shut your mouth, and kiss me."

He could not help but loose a whoop of excitement. They flung themselves at one another, tackling in mid-flight and rolling to the pallet, which smelled of pure Lightning and no tainted roses. Traveler's lips were on Lightning's before they had landed properly, and they drank deep before roving over his neck, his throat, his collarbone, his face.

Lightning moaned, a sound Traveler had greatly missed. "Too -- too many clothes," he whispered. "Bare us."

Traveler whispered a word of power, and the garments vanished from their bodies, boots to collar. And oh, but Lightning had had the right idea. Skin against skin felt ever much better, good enough to bring his cock upright with a violent jerk. Grinding his pelvis against Lightning's, he felt a matching wood there, arching up against him.

Lightning gave a startled, amused half-laugh. "So there he is. I tried, Traveler, when you were gone, to remember you and your touch, but --"

"Shh." Traveler kissed Lightning's lips again, silencing him. "We were meant to be together. One is not whole without the other. Now, I believe you said something about silence?"

His Gypsy mate's laugh filled out warm and true as summer sunshine. Lightning kissed Traveler in kind, playing wicked games with his tongue until both were laughing at their foolishness, then abandoned games for the sake of ravishing each other's bodies. They writhed and bucked, hands roaming wherever hands could roam, fingers sliding over heavy cocks and sneaking into the creases of their arses.

Traveler spared a thought for the notion of Lightning taking control one day. The idea inflamed him so that he pinned Lightning flat and kissed his Gypsy's breath away. Lightning moaned and thrashed with ecstasy, which gave Traveler another idea...

Pushing and shoving Lightning onto his stomach, Traveler parted the youth's quivering arse cheeks wide and plunged in with his tongue. He lapped at the hole, getting reacquainted with Lightning's savory flavor, then pushed inside the tight muscle again and again until Lightning's cries grew frantic.

Oil. They needed oil. Traveler searched the caravan with his thoughts, and found a near-empty flask with other foodstuffs. The amount was little, but would suffice. He called the flask to him, warmed it with a thought, and splashed near half against Lightning's entrance.

Ah, and it was a pleasure to hear Lightning yelp, to see him squirm and push back as Traveler opened him with fingers and worked the oil in well.

Traveler used the rest of the oil to anoint his pulsing cock, and placed its head to Lightning's hole. "I cannot wait," he whispered, breaking the rule of silence.

"Nor I. Now, Traveler. Now, now, now...!"

Both near-keened as Traveler thrust past the tight muscle and to the scalding heat within. Lightning spasmed as he was speared, and began to hump against the pallet. Traveler would have lifted the youth and used his own hand on Lightning's prick, but Lords, he hadn't the patience or strength. Instead, he fucked his mate hard, riding him rough as a stallion while in his turn, Lightning bucked against him and into the pallet.

Their noise would have woken the dead -- aye, and made them cackle with glee or clap their bony hands.

Traveler felt pressure building hard and fast in his balls. He would have regretted it's coming so soon, but for sure and certain there would be plenty of other occasions where he could take his time. "Now," he groaned. "You too, Lightning, please..."

Lightning screamed and pumped his hips as Traveler came, and so did he. Their shared orgasm went on for far longer than was natural, pleasure building beyond what man was meant to enjoy, but neither held back morsel or whit. They clung together for the ride, so long as it might last.

When Traveler came back to himself, he was draped over Lightning like a blanket. Lightning bore his weight for a moment only, then bucked against him with a different intent. "Off, you crate of bricks. I'll smother, so I will."

Chuckling, Traveler pulled his half-softened cock from Lightning's hole. They wrestled a bit, both playing like boys until Traveler had dragged Lightning down against him, Lightning's back to his chest, and could hold tight.

They rested a bit, sweat cooling and labored breathing easing.

"And what will we do now?" Lightning echoed Traveler's earlier question. "You and I, what comes next in our *own* story?"

"Freedom, for one."

"Aye? How do you mean?"

"Mmm." Traveler tucked his chin against Lightning's stubbly scalp. "I've a plan in mind, I do, and I think you'll like it passing well..."

"Does it involve leaving these faire grounds? They're a foul place for us Gypsies, and I'll be glad to be quit of them."

"We will leave, for sure and certain, this

very day if you like. Though I think things will improve for our kin now Rosalind can no longer play her games. I'm certain she's the nasty force behind the ill-doing on these Grounds."

"Bitch," Lightning snarled. "But go on. What would your plan be?"

"Kiss me, and I'll tell you."

Lightning squirmed about in Traveler's arms until they were face to face, and laid his sweet lips over Traveler's. He sparkled as he drew back. "Trade and trade about."

"My own," Traveler murmured. "I'll give you my plan, and we'll see what you make of what I have in mind..."

Epilogue

Traveler finished his stoking of their fire -- with*out* magic, as Lightning insisted he must not depend on it for simple things they could do themselves. Ah, but they'd wrangled about that more than a bit, but in the end Traveler gave way. A little hard work would do him no harm.

When he said as much to Lightning, Lightning had looked smug as a cat.

He sat back on his heels to examine the hearth. It had been good craftsmanship when he'd built his home on the island, stone by stone fixed in place with his own two hands, and the construction pleased him still.

Aye, well and well, Lightning did have something to his notions about leaving magic lie when one's own effort served equally good.

He'd not admit it again, though, for Lightning would tease him without mercy.

Traveler stood from where he'd been crouched on his haunches and faced Lightning. As ever, even after the better part of a year, Lightning's beauty stole his breath. Particularly when he was in this sort of mood, which had apparently prompted him to shed all his clothes and stretch out naked on the dais bed.

Lightning languidly raised one arm above his head and let his thighs fall apart. "Are you seeing something you like?"

"Minx. You know I do, and I'll be taking as much as I please in a bit. But first, I would know your final opinion."

"On what?" Lightning asked with a wicked smile.

"Minx and imp both, I'll be bound. How does my plan suit you? Fair seasons on the road, and wintering here on my island. We've traveled from here to there and back again, and now we're set for the snows. Are you content?"

"I think I may be." Luck and Patpaw, both fat from a healthy diet of mice and careless birds, swarmed up onto the dais for petting and the adoration they both surely felt they deserved. Patpaw had recovered from her shame over being used as a tool, and now her purrs were loud enough to hear even by the hearth. "Are my two horses and Thundercloud stabled well?"

"Well as horses may be, with plenty of good clean hay to eat, warm under blankets. I repeat myself: are you content?"

"Hmm. In truth, I'll confess I have wandered enough to hold me for a while, and we have even heard from Meilin."

"'Tis good to know he's doing well. Though I'll be switched if his letter isn't full of riddles as the man himself."

Lightning shrugged. "Such is Meilin's way. Now, where was I? Ah, yes. We've traveled long and well, and made it far enough East to replenish my stocks of tea." He pinned Traveler with a severe look. "Which you will not be duplicating with magic, understood? It's bad enough I let you come with me into the secret groves."

"No, Master," Traveler mocked with good humor. "Though you can't stop me from planting trees and bushes in my gardens, where all things grow so well without the aid of magic."

"How does that come about, by the bye?"

"The ground likes me. I treat it well."

"Mmm, as you treat so well all things you care for." Lightning wickedly began to stroke his cock, already a hard and tempting treat lying flush against his belly. "I'm satisfied with our bargain, my Traveler."

"Good." Traveler began to prowl toward the dais bed. "Now, let me satisfy you with something else."

Lightning chortled as Traveler swept the cats aside and pounced on him. "My love," he said fondly as Traveler rose above him.

"My Lightning, my Thorn, my dearest, my own. Kiss me to seal our pact."

Their lips pressed one against the other, and they were content.

* * *

And somewhere, in a place they could not ken, Meilin, otherwise known as a Lord of the Road, albeit the most humble of all, found himself suffused with a sure and certain peace and *smiled*...

Faire Grounds

Printed in the United States
117562LV00001B/7/A